BRIMSTONE 1

ENDORSEMENTS

Be warned: clear your schedule and prepare to get no sleep before you read the first page of *Brimstone 1*. Author Jason Karpf, who was raised in Hollywood, knows a thing or two about creating electrifying drama and action. Karpf puts his considerable skillset to good use as he harkens us back to the thrill of classic science fiction but with a contemporary faith-based twist. Bring on *Brimstone 2*!
—**Lee Purcell**, actress/producer, two-time Emmy nominee

From *Jeopardy* champion to renowned writer, Jason Karpf is widely recognized for his polymathic capacities. His gripping new novel, *Brimstone 1*, brings together his unique knowledge of history, politics, technology, and Scripture to create a compelling narrative. Highly recommended!
—**James Strock**, author of *Serve to Lead, Reagan on Leadership*

In the realm of *Contact* and *Arrival, Brimstone 1* is a classic good vs. evil story. Its explosive ending is as satisfying as a good burger and shake.
—**David Price**, writer/producer, director of *Children of the Corn II, Dr. Jekyll and Ms. Hyde*

BRIMSTONE 1

Jason William Karpf

ELK LAKE PUBLISHING INC
PUBLISHING THE POSITIVE
Plymouth, Massachusetts

COPYRIGHT

Brimstone 1

Cover and Interior Design: Derinda Babcock
Editor(s): Judy Hagey, Deb Haggerty
PUBLISHED BY: Elk Lake Publishing, Inc., 35 Dogwood Drive, Plymouth, MA 02360, 2021

Library Cataloging Data

Names: Karpf, Jason William (Jason William Karpf)

Brimstone 1 / Jason William Karpf

234 p. 23cm × 15cm (9in × 6 in.)

Identifiers: ISBN-13: 978-1-64949-137-4 (paperback) | 978-1-64949-138-1 (trade hardcover) | 978-1-64949-237-1 (hardcover)| 978-1-64949-219-7 (e-book)

Key Words: Suspense/thriller, rockets, domestic terrorism, aliens and UFOs, futuristic, outer space, speculative

LCCN: 2021930200 Fiction

Ask me and I will tell you remarkable secrets you do not know about things to come.—Jeremiah 33:3

CHAPTER 1

"The voice of one crying in the wilderness."

Elijah Lindstrom knew this barren stretch, but this was the first time he'd disturbed its soil. Until now, he had practiced his path in virtual reality, growing familiar with the outcroppings and fissures. He ran gloved fingertips over a slab of rose-colored stone and spoke into the headset mic again, "Target confirmed, per mapping."

Conventional wisdom called for crew, hardware, and time to divine the rocky terrain's secrets. Elijah had abandoned those for artificial intelligence, opting to analyze sites around the planet. He had found a way to predict which formations held back seeps from deep, distant reservoirs. No need for traditional equipment as he was not leading a convoy of six-wheeled vehicles to crawl the terrain for seismic soundings.

He removed and unzipped his quiver. "Fly, my doves."

With a flip of his hand, he released a bevy of small drones. They assumed a triangular formation, with the fourth and largest hovering in the middle. Rotors on the lead machine reversed, prompting a drop to the desert floor. The tungsten striker on its underside shot a tuned sonic wave into the ground. Its smaller siblings took readings and sent them to the tablet Elijah held. On a server twelve hundred miles away, AI programs crunched the readings and returned sonar resolutions.

BRIMSTONE 1

Elijah wiped a layer of fine, red dust from the tablet and assessed the coalescing pictures. The sturdy lead drone rebounded from its controlled crash and repeated the sounding drop at different locations, the other three keeping station above.

Elijah had planned his excursion with the intensity of a spacewalk. This expanse of southern New Mexico was an alien world to him. Little changed since Coronado's exploration, even with the technology of the twenty-first century's third decade, the landscape was still intimidating—a land for the lost. Following a timeline predating the conquistadors by millions of years, he sought hydrocarbons, increasingly unpopular as an energy source but far from obsolete. The discovery of overlooked shale oil deposits spurred him to develop proprietary hardware and software, make the long drive from North Dakota, and trespass.

Elijah's adrenaline rose with the early readings. A potential oil pocket cast a tantalizing shadow on his display. The throb in the air didn't register for a few crucial seconds. By the time Elijah looked up, the Subaru Bell helicopter was closing fast from the east. In reflex, he checked his smart watch, confirming he was still within the margin of safety for security response time, per recent social media chatter. He'd expected a few more minutes to study the strata.

Elijah sheathed his tablet and started running. His drones, programmed to return if Elijah's smart watch read sudden movement, swooped home, and latched back in the quiver with their tiny metal claws.

He stopped to catch his breath and assess his pursuit. The helicopter hovered, stalking him. His truck waited under a camo tarp, tucked in an arroyo a quarter mile away. His long legs started pumping.

Elijah charged into a line of sagebrush, hoping the plants would provide cover. The path to his truck lay ahead, bisected by a dirt road. A plume rose at the far end of the road—a black Suburban rumbling in his direction. He was pinned.

Within the tangle of sagebrush, he moved away from the approaching vehicle and his truck. Branches jabbed his face and tore at his clothes. He cursed his recklessness.

There is more hope for fools than for people who think they are wise. Elijah first learned the verse as a show-off in youth group who liked to answer every question first. He stumbled out of the vegetation. The converging engines roared ever louder, and he fell to his hands and knees. A pair of boots entered his field of vision.

"Don't let the man getcha." A calloused hand pulled Elijah to his feet.

He's too old to be a security officer. Elijah decided to trust the man and followed him up a rugged incline.

Boulders crowded the path, yet Elijah's new guide threaded them like he was walking across his front yard. The rocks grew taller until they tapered into hoodoos. The stand of natural columns made a good hiding place, but the old man forged ahead. As Elijah looked skyward toward the racket of the helicopter, the ground came out from under him.

The old man croaked with laughter as Elijah tumbled into a crevasse shielded by the hoodoos. The pair continued into the shadows. Elijah clicked on a penlight. The helicopter's roar muted as the pair descended the cavern.

The old man gazed at the cavern ceiling as if he were seeing through the limestone. "They'll be gone soon." He switched on a battery-powered lantern.

A walk-in time capsule unfolded. Framed movie posters leaned against the walls, primarily biblical epics—*The Robe, Quo Vadis, The Ten Commandments.* A Motorola Calypso portable record player sat next to milk crates full of vintage vinyl albums. Webbed lawn chairs and folding cots added the final homey touch.

The old man gestured for him to take a seat. Elijah slid the quiver off his tired shoulder, dropped the rest of gear, and settled gingerly into one of the rickety lawn chairs.

"Hungry?" The man retrieved a can from a stack of corroded containers and drums.

Elijah took the item politely. Faded lettering foretold the contents of the can, chopped ham and eggs, while the small-print expiration date suggested something less appetizing—February 1959. "Nice man cave," he said, trying to calm himself.

Another croaking laugh. "Any teenager would want to ride out World War III in style. My dad worked on the Manhattan Project. I told him it was his fault I'd have to live in a hole in the ground."

Elijah hefted the civilian defense ration. "Still expecting the end of the world?"

"Not the end. Rebirth." The old man sat on the lawn chair opposite Elijah and looked him in the eye. "The time's coming. That's why you were poking around." He leaned toward him. "Outer space. The Word of God," he whispered. "Eighty years in the making. You know what I'm talking about, don't you?"

Elijah shook his head, puzzled. "Really? Then what's this stuff for?" He jumped from his chair, unzipped Elijah's quiver, and glanced appreciatively at the contents. "Drones? Fancy design."

Surprised by the old man's agility, Elijah took the quiver from him. "Thanks. My design." He collected he remainder of his equipment. "But I'm looking for oil, not aliens."

Elijah had no interest being trapped underground with a jumping hermit spouting Area 51 tales. He turned. The man was gone. Behind the pyramid of survival stores sat a second tunnel, pitch black. The old man must have slipped into the passageway while Elijah collected his equipment. He paused, then opted for the route known to lead to daylight.

Elijah emerged slowly from the crevasse, crept back through the hoodoos, and then jogged to his concealed truck. No sign of security or the old man. Soon, Elijah was bouncing down the arroyo toward a dirt road and eventually a county highway. He checked his rearview mirror—no helicopters or flying saucers. He threw his head back and whooped.

Todos Santos, the local population center, boasted one big-box store. Interrupting the strip malls were a few examples of WPA architecture—Works Progress Administration—government largesse from Franklin Roosevelt's time in office. Aping the adobe revival structures was a complex of apartments, relics themselves from the more recent 1980s, still splashed with salmon and turquoise. Weary, Elijah pulled into a guest parking spot.

"You're late, bro," Brad Ferris said without looking up at the sound of his front door opening. Sprawled on the couch, Brad alternated binge watching on the big screen, checking storyline information for his show on his tablet, and responding to a text on his phone.

"Didn't plan on traffic. Big accident outside of Pueblo," Elijah set down his bags.

"You look like a big accident. Did you drive across the desert or crawl?" Brad appraised Elijah streaked with dirt and sweat. The two young men laughed and hugged. "Thought you were gonna make me look like an idiot by missing the meeting with Mr. Moore."

"No, I'll make you look like an idiot by taking the meeting," Elijah said. "Maybe make him look like one too."

"You sure?" Brad pulled two cans of flavored seltzer from the fridge and tossed one to Elijah.

"He'll find nothing the way he's going," Elijah said. "I haven't seen you post any pictures of gushers on Moore social media, right?"

"Hardly." Brad flopped back on the couch. "I hope you'll also have some good news for him."

"The part I didn't put in the report yet"—Elijah tugged at his quiver—"I sank my last five hundred bucks into upgraded circuits. We're ready for our demo."

"Sorry you're tapped out," said Brad. "You have gas money to get home?"

"That would show lack of faith about tomorrow." Elijah cocked an eyebrow.

"You really want your meeting to go well?" Brad made a show of sniffing the air. "Take a shower!"

Later that evening, alone in the spare bedroom, Elijah checked his data from his brief drone deployment. All was intact, automatically saved when the motion detectors in his watch had sensed him running—his "trouble" program. He readied for his nightly ritual. Lying on the sleeper sofa with his tablet cradled on his knees, he opened an encrypted app. Moore Ranch Mysteries was a web chat dedicated to the vast property surrounding Todos Santos, the private land where Elijah had fled security that afternoon. The app drew trolls, conspiracy theorists, and curious lurkers. Framed in slick graphics, the platform suggested a digital ghost town.

Elijah scrolled various topic categories—3 Generations of Con Men, Christian Conspiracy, No Oil—until he arrived at Security Team Response Time. A thread of posts provided anecdotes from trespassers on how long Moore security took to engage them. Elijah tapped an entry using his community handle.

JustCurious: 11 minutes.

In the master bedroom with the door closed, Brad sat at a small desk. He had the administrator's view of the Moore Ranch Mysteries app. Elijah's new post triggered an alert as did any statement about intrusion on the ranch. Brad tried to track the post's origin, despite the app's promise of encryption and anonymity for users. The author was using a quality VPN, his digital tracks covered. Brad smirked.

A chat window appeared in the corner of Brad's screen: "Do you know who '11 minutes' is?"

"Maybe," Brad typed back.

The next morning, Elijah finalized his interview look in the bathroom mirror, tightening his black hair into a semi-bun, setting a conservative stud in his earlobe. Once outside, he sealed the quiver holding his drones in the cargo box inside his Ram 1500's rear fender. If the meeting went well, he would present his technology. Doing so at this point would be pretentious.

Taking the county highway out of Todos Santos, Elijah passed another WPA landmark. He slowed to read the sign: KNMR, Birthplace of Moore Media. The radio station sat several hundred yards off the road, a low structure with earthen walls and exposed timbers, protected by a tall, wrought iron fence. The original broadcast tower gleamed over the site. Cresting a rise, Elijah spotted the descendants of the tower, a cluster of monstrous dishes beaming in all directions, the sprawling, electronic heart of the Moore Media empire. The ranch entrance was still several miles away on a private road that branched off the highway.

Elijah checked in at the main gate and arrived at Moore headquarters, an office park in what had been rangeland. A central office building dominated the complex with a sprawling low-slung structure under construction nearby, signage announcing the future home of the Moore Museum of Christian Broadcasting.

Elijah made one more security stop in the foyer of the main building and took the short elevator ride to the executive floor. The upper lobby served as an archive of the Moore family's decades of accomplishments. A photo gallery included Baxter Moore, the first, and his wife, Marge, with Bing Crosby at their Albuquerque station in 1947; Baxter, the second, performing at a Jesus Music festival in 1971 as Billy Graham looked on; and Baxter, the third, touring Google's then-headquarters with Larry Page and Sergey Brin in 1999.

On the lobby's back wall was a huge mosaic of colored stones and polished metal, the seal of Moore Media. The circular design contained images representing radio, television, publishing and music—heroic, stylized images of looming transmission towers, broadcast waves resembling lightning, glowing cathode ray tubes, a mammoth press spouting print material, an instrument cluster of silver trumpet, golden harp, and cherry-red electric guitar. A cruciform separated the business unit quadrants. Scripture ran along the bottom:

Isaiah 52:7 (RSV)
How beautiful upon the mountains
are the feet of him who brings good tidings,
who publishes peace, who brings good tidings of good,
who publishes salvation,
who says to Zion, "Your God reigns."

Intrigued by the ornate slab, Elijah flinched at an unexpected voice in his ear. "My grandfather commissioned it just before he died in 1975. I added the border in 1999." The words were soft and reverent.

Elijah followed the pointing hand thrust over his shoulder and squinted at the ribbon of black stone with silver inlay. The detail was a WAN diagram, a wide array network, a repeating array of linked computers, relays, routers, and servers encircling the depictions of traditional media.

Elijah turned to face the man behind him. "The age of the internet."

The man smiled at Elijah's grasp of the symbolism. "Mr. Lindstrom, I'm Baxter Moore." He gave Elijah a vigorous handshake.

America's twenty-third richest person did not match Elijah's suit-and-tie take on the day. Baxter sported the same business casual uniform—polo shirt and khakis—he wore in the photo at early Google. His hair had invariably thinned and grayed, but his wiry frame hadn't required a bump in clothing sizes in the last quarter-century.

Baxter motioned for Elijah to follow as he strode down the hall. Flatscreens displayed broadcasts and clips from the wealth of Moore Media content.

"Busy morning ... launching a web network for Indonesia. Hundreds of languages and dialects. Hundreds of millions of people needing the gospel." Baxter pointed to a screen with the Indonesian feed.

"And now you want to get into the oil business?"

"According to you, I'm not getting into it any time soon." Baxter led Elijah into a conference room and shut the door.

"I said a lot of things in my report." Elijah pulled his tablet out of his briefcase. "Frankly, sir, I thought at best I'd get a webcall with your petroleum geologist. Let me repeat, this is an honor."

"Your old buddy Brad Ferris is doing a great job as our digital marketing director. He knows my door is always open." Baxter took his seat at the head of the table. "So after you sent him your report, it landed in my inbox. Your work is impressive, even if it says I'm crazy." Baxter's gracious smile had not dimmed, but Elijah's heart still raced.

"You've been drilling in locations with appropriate thermal maturity," Elijah said. "Textbook approach." Elijah synced his tablet to the media wall and displayed charts from the report he'd sent to the Moore organization.

"Our analysis says we should reach shale deposits eventually," Baxter interjected.

"No," Elijah countered, "as I said in my report, you have a false positive just like the case study I included about the Caspian Horizon project in Kazakhstan. Your drill sites here in New Mexico have all the same characteristics. Promising at first, but you'll hit magma before you find good shale."

Elijah expanded images and charts from the failed Kazakhstan exploration. Baxter thumbed through a stack of printouts. He stopped at Elijah's résumé.

"University of North Dakota, Master's in Petroleum Engineering, 2022. Certification in Robotics"—Baxter read off the résumé—"Good credentials, but I have people who were in the biz before you were born."

"Caspian Horizon's project lead was sixty-three years old, published author, award-winner. Experienced people can be wrong," responded Elijah.

"Back in Williston, did you tell David Colton he was wrong too? You like kicking big shots in the shins?" Baxter tapped Elijah's work experience page.

"I left Colton Engineering because Dave and I had a disagreement on patents."

"Sometimes you have to be flexible, think long-term. Mr. Colton is a major operator and a believer."

"No doubt on the first point."

Baxter gave a short whistle after the comment before returning to the résumé. "Your objective says, 'Seeking a petroleum engineering position with a Christ-centered organization.' You'd like to work for me."

"Yes, sir. You're one of the most Christ-centered business leaders in the country. And I admire your plans to use RF technology to crack the shale instead of traditional fracking methods."

"We'll start with fracking, but radio waves are more environmentally friendly than pumping water, especially when they're powered by solar panels and waste gas," Baxter said. "Or do you think it hypocritical to bring up the environment in any discussion of fossil fuels?"

"Environmental stewardship is mandatory everywhere. Fossil fuels aren't going away yet. Just like beef. I'm showing my North Dakota roots, I know." Elijah smiled. He always enjoyed giving his enlightened take on petroleum.

"Now, suppose I overlook your badmouthing a former employer and hire you," Baxter continued. "Why join an outfit specializing in dry holes?"

"Because you have excellent odds of finding shale deposits on your land—if you look in the right places." Elijah kept steady but Baxter's jabs rattled him. Proverbs 26:12 echoed the same as when security chased him.

Baxter clapped his hands. "And you know the right places?"

"I have a good idea."

"You have x-ray vision?"

"Next best thing. Heat flow spectrography using secondary sources."

"That's a holy grail, if you've solved it," Baxter leaned back in his chair. "Indulge me. Tell me how you're doing this."

"Picture a satellite that didn't hit its mark. It's orbiting too low and pointing the wrong direction. The satellite was supposed to find atmospheric biosignatures on exoplanets," Elijah said. "Instead, it's finding interesting emissions on Mother Earth."

"Interesting indeed, especially for the satellite investors hoping to salvage their bust," Baxter said. "We'd still need old-fashioned confirmation on the ground. I could bring back survey teams myself. Of course, that would take a few years and a few more truckloads of money. You know how big the Moore Ranch is."

Elijah shook his head. "Second holy grail. Surveys finished in a matter of weeks, cheaper than you can imagine."

Baxter stared at Elijah. The young man returned the gaze. The conference call speaker trilled.

"Mr. Moore, Carla Webster," Baxter's admin said over the speaker.

"On-screen please." Baxter motioned for Elijah to stay in the room while he took the call. The image of a woman at a desk replaced Elijah's presentation on the conference room screen.

"We just got word. Mrs. Garcia is going to be all right," Carla said. "They stopped the bleeding, and the baby is fine."

"Praise Jesus!" Baxter pumped his fist. Elijah manipulated the presentation on his tablet while the conversation continued.

"The doctor has ordered complete bedrest for the remainder of the pregnancy," continued Carla. "It leaves us without a science teacher for the rest of the term. But if that's the worst news we get today—"

"Amen. Update the students and staff." Baxter looked at Elijah who was still engrossed with his tablet. "I'll get back to you about finding a substitute teacher." Baxter ended the call and rose.

"Mr. Lindstrom, you've given me plenty to think about. But I intend to stick with our current drilling plan. That said, you're hired."

Elijah stood, confused. Baxter waved Elijah's résumé.

"Among your many accomplishments, I see you've taught science at Christian camps and math on mission trips," Baxter said. "As we just heard, they're short one science teacher at Jeshimon Academy, our school in Todos Santos. We'll need you from now through June."

The unexpected offer stung Elijah. His hometown friends had worked fast food during high school and college. He'd taught kids. Now he had his master's degree and was determined to pursue his career in engineering with no intention of going back to his version of flipping burgers. "Mr. Moore, I came here to talk about finding oil."

"You said you wanted to work for me. Very few people get invited to the ranch. Fewer still get to join the Moore team." Baxter smiled.

Elijah forced a laugh. "I'd be a fool to say no." He hoped Baxter wouldn't sense his ambivalence.

"You're no fool." Baxter clasped Elijah on the shoulder. "My executive admin, Donna, will connect you with Mrs. Webster at the school. I'll circle back with you in a bit."

Baxter's smart watch vibrated. He glanced at the text on his wrist while guiding Elijah to the conference room door.

JULIUS: On my way.

Once Elijah left the conference room, Baxter closed the door and retreated to a far alcove. He touched a biometric sensor, opened a concealed door, and left the room.

Baxter threaded a passage to a service stairwell. Soon he was downstairs and exiting the building from a side door. An orange Bronco with roof and doors removed, ubiquitous Moore logo on the hood, lurched to a stop.

"You hired him?" The man behind the wheel emulated Baxter's business casual dress with the addition of a sport coat, keeping his Jericho PL .40 caliber discreet in its shoulder holster.

"Julius, I appreciate you driving over to express your displeasure," Baxter said. "You Brits are so proper."

"He's most likely a spy," Julius said. "We're still enhancing video from the helicopter, but the intruder is looking very much like your new science teacher. I'll run it in your office."

"Later." Baxter settled in the passenger seat. "I want to drop by Rig Alpha."

Julius gunned the Bronco out of the parking lot onto a dirt road. "He fits our threat profile. Comes from an observant family that suffered tragedy. Has conflict with Christian authority figures. We dug up more emails of the row he had with David Colton."

"I jabbed him on that, just like you suggested," Baxter said. "You heard how he barely stayed cool."

"Colton is a prominent Christian philanthropist. Lindstrom called him a liar 'hiding behind the cross.' Now he's submitted a document basically calling you a failure. See the pattern?"

"And we have the perfect way to watch him," Baxter replied. "Your people can do a complete background check, legally. Now when he sneaks back to the ranch, don't crowd him."

"Let him get cocky." Julius accepted Baxter's strategy.

"You know what I'm really afraid of?" Baxter said. "That he's telling the truth. Then we *will* have to get into the oil business."

CHAPTER 2

"You must've really impressed Mr. Moore." Carla Webster, the principal, walked Elijah out of the administration building toward the gym. Jeshimon Academy was the crown jewel of Todos Santos's WPA architecture, the one-time public high school now a private Christian campus, a mashup of rough adobe textures and art moderne geometries.

"He makes the big impression," Elijah said.

Carla laughed and nodded. She plucked her vibrating phone from a pocket, looked at the screen, and smiled. "The director of the camp where you taught," she said before reading the message aloud: "'Elijah is brilliant. He relates wonderfully to young people. He explains complex subjects in a friendly manner. Call anytime for more details.'"

"Things move fast around here," Elijah said.

"You get used to the pace when you work for the Moore organization."

"Is he a tough boss?"

"Not as tough as the crew you're about to meet." Carla pushed open the metal door to the gym.

With the bleachers retracted and the basketball standards folded toward the ceiling, the court provided maximum space for the throng of teenage students. They bunched at their robotics projects, adjusting and commanding their machines, an occasional yell punctuating the din.

Carla directed Elijah to stand with her on a bench where a portable PA waited.

"Students, may I have your attention," Carla said into the mic. "This is Mr. Lindstrom. Mr. Moore sent him over as a substitute for Mrs. Garcia. Let's try not to scare him off on the first day."

The gathering students laughed as Carla turned the mic over to Elijah. "Hello, everyone. Mrs. Webster told me you have a robotics competition coming up. I've been in quite a few myself."

"How many did you win?" a student shouted, triggering more laughter.

"Seven." The students whooped appreciatively. "I'd like to visit each team and see how you're doing."

The students returned to their groups as Elijah shed his jacket and tie. As he stepped off the bench, he rolled up his sleeves, revealing tattoos on his forearms, including his life verse, Jeremiah 33:3.

"Mr. Lindstrom, would you like to see the winning entry first?" A sixteen-year-old girl with red curls approached Elijah with a stack of binders. Her teammates laughed nervously. "Our team is 'Thy Kingdom Code.'"

"So you think you've got this wrapped up? The Bible warns about boasting." Elijah felt the irony of warning someone about flashing their intellect.

"Scripture also tells us to be bold." The girl handed over a meticulous engineering notebook with supplements. "I'm Shiloh."

Elijah nodded and skimmed the notebook. "Your team is building a home health aide."

"Yes, the robot dispenses medicine, conducts wellness checks based on the patient's verbal responses, and can take vitals and relay them to doctors." Shiloh's excitement grew. "I got the idea when my grandma got sick and ..."

"You're overheating," Elijah said. Shiloh stopped her pitch, apparently confused. Elijah wafted the air with his hand. "Smell that? The cortex is running hot. You have about fifteen seconds to shut it down ... voluntarily."

Shiloh inhaled. She ran back to her group. Elijah calmly followed her to Thy Kingdom Code's pit area.

"Could be a bad wire. Could be your program is straining the hardware," Elijah explained. "Let me know what you find."

Continuing to the other pits, Elijah met with each team, perusing their notebooks, watching their robots in action, and commenting on their projects. The afternoon went quickly, the students excited by the new teacher's ideas and energy. The spirit filled Elijah as well. The students were smart and grateful. He'd made inroads with Baxter Moore. He was on the inside. All good, he kept telling himself. The bell rang to end the school day, and the students packed their gear.

"Shiloh, will you pray us out?" Elijah requested.

"Heavenly Father, we thank you that Mrs. Garcia and her baby are going to be all right," Students murmured affirmation. "Thank you for sending Mr. Lindstrom. Please watch over him as he watches over us. All this we pray in your name."

A unison amen, and the students filed out of the gym. A beaming Carla came alongside Elijah.

"I've updated Mr. Moore on the incredible work you did today," Carla said.

"I wouldn't call it work"—Elijah retrieved his coat and tie—"I love robots."

"Mr. Moore has another position for you while you teach. It's part-time," Carla said. Elijah perked up. Maybe this offer had to do with the oil program. "School caretaker. We've been needing someone to keep an eye on the campus, do light repairs."

Elijah hung back a step as Carla walked him across the basketball court to a hallway. He didn't want his face to betray his deflation. "Here's the best part," she said. "Free room and board."

A narrow staircase led to an efficiency apartment in the gym's basement. The space included a kitchenette, a battered desk and dresser, and a bare mattress. Elijah mustered a smile. “The price is right,” he said.

“Elijah, I know why you came here,” Carla said. “Maybe your prayers weren’t answered today, but you answered ours. Can I get you to sign our employee agreement?”

Carla held out a tablet displaying a contract. Elijah speed-read the document—compensation, job descriptions for teacher and caretaker, permission to conduct a background check, and lifestyle requirements including no sex outside of marriage and no alcohol. He scrawled a signature with his index finger.

“And one more thing. Consider it a hiring bonus.” Carla presented Elijah a prepaid debit card and extended an arm for a hug. Elijah accepted both.

Elijah returned to his apartment that evening, arms filled with shopping bags. He dropped his bed-in-a-bag on the mattress and began sorting housewares and canned food in the kitchenette. His phone sounded with an incoming video call.

“Hey, Mom,” Elijah propped the phone on the counter as he resumed organizing.

“I know you texted everything is fine. We didn’t mean to bother you.” Teri Lindstrom called out to her husband across the house. “Duane, are you on?”

“You’re no bother. I should’ve called already.” Elijah glanced back at the phone screen as he stocked his shelves.

“I’m here,” Duane said. The call from North Dakota split into two images. Elijah’s father logged in from a desktop in the bedroom.

“Have you seen the lesson plans?” Teri said.

“Yes. Mrs. Garcia’s plans are great.” Elijah faced the phone. “The textbook publishers have a lot of resources online too.” He turned back to his canned vegetables and ramen packets.

“Teaching job,” Duane sneered. “If you wanted to teach so bad, your mom could’ve set you up right here in town.”

"We all know I didn't come down here looking for a teaching assignment," Elijah said over his shoulder. "It just happened."

"Good thing since your big move with Baxter Moore went bust. You didn't need to run away from Williston for an oil job either." Duane began coughing.

"I didn't run away," Elijah said. "I've been working on this for a long time."

"We're proud," Teri said. "God sent you to those students."

"He obviously didn't send you there to find the next Bakken play." Duane reached for a pill bottle near his monitor as his coughing increased.

"God tell you that himself?" Elijah faced the phone again.

"That's enough, both of you," Teri said.

"Takes a man to admit game over." Duane fumbled with the safety lid. "If you were smart, you'd come home."

"About as likely as you going back to the fields," Elijah said.

Duane's face tightened in fury. The pill bottle popped from his hands and hit the floor. He pushed away from the web camera, his wheelchair now in view. He jostled a joystick, trying to command a mechanical arm mounted on the side of his chair, cursing between coughs.

"Dad, the new unit is more sensitive. Center the joystick, move it slowly," Elijah said, softening as he watched his father struggle.

Duane got the arm to extend and retrieve the pill bottle with its sensor-tipped claw. He wheeled out of frame without a glance toward the camera or a goodbye.

"Another lung infection," Teri said, her eyes red-rimmed. "They seem to be getting worse."

"The guys from church will take my stuff to the shipping place. I boxed everything before I left," Elijah said.

Teri nodded. "I love you."

"Love you too, Mom." The screen went black.

Elijah returned to his kitchenette setup. He extracted a ladle from a utensil set and lathered it with dish soap. A moment later, he twirled the ladle into the sink and sent the unpacked remainder of the set flying. He leaned on the counter and exhaled, the faucet still running. Elijah wanted to blame the Enemy for driving him to anger throughout this important day. As usual, he blamed himself for being weak, easily goaded. The phone sounded again, this time with the assigned ringtone for Brad. Elijah read the text:

Brad: All hands on deck at the ranch studio. Prayer vigil for the new web channel and believers in Indonesia. PS—be ready to meet a celeb.

Ninety minutes later, Elijah arrived at the ranch studio, Moore Media's flagship facility with a global newsroom and a stage. The studio was rarely used to full capacity as talent usually preferred the company's sites in Albuquerque, Nashville, or Jerusalem. But when Moore Media had a major announcement, the ranch was the origin point.

Elijah entered the audience area, the tiered seating filling with Moore staffers and guests. Brad sat at the end of a row, updating social media on a tablet with an attached keyboard.

"Good day?" Brad asked.

"Right up to the part when my dad got on the phone," Elijah said.

"My dad said he'd call me after his honeymoon. That was ... six years ago?" Brad laughed. "Maybe he's mad I didn't get him a wedding gift."

The lights dimmed and the stage manager counted down to broadcast. Baxter took the stage as the audience applauded.

"Hello, I'm Baxter Moore, CEO of Moore Media. Welcome to our prayer vigil for Indonesia. This morning, we launched a web network for believers in that great nation, believers today and believers tomorrow. We have guests around the world ready to talk and sing about their love for Indonesia and our mission there."

Huge screens showed live vigils and worship on multiple continents. "We'll start with words of inspiration right here at Moore Ranch Studios," Baxter said. "Please welcome a daughter of Christ and an American hero, Jana McAlister."

Jana walked out of the wings to a standing ovation. The screens displayed a montage of her distinguished moments: standing beside an F-35 on a carrier deck, giving a thumbs up with a gloved hand en route to the International Space Station, teaching young students in a classroom, extolling a megachurch congregation. She had traded her flight suit for a Ralph Lauren blazer and Tony Lama boots with Christian crosses stitched into the leather, her current image of command. Jana embraced Baxter and waved to the audience.

Elijah clapped enthusiastically. Brad gave him a sly look as the ovation subsided. "Good little Christian nerd. You had her picture on your wall when you were thirteen," he said into Elijah's ear.

"Good little preacher's kid. Your walls were bare," Elijah retorted.

Baxter and Jana took seats in a talk show set on the stage. "Jana, how many countries have you seen?" Baxter said.

"I've lost count." Jana smiled. "Any that I missed in the navy, I saw from outer space." Baxter and the audience laughed.

"The Great Commission tells us to baptize and teach all nations," Baxter said. "What does that mean to you?"

"It means God's love is for everyone," Jana said. "His Son died for everyone. But forty-two percent of the world hasn't heard the name 'Jesus.' If they don't hear his name, if they don't learn his ways, how will they know that love? How will they be saved?"

"How have you carried out the Great Commission?"

"In the navy, I led life groups on ships and at bases. Very important to stay in the Word no matter where you are."

"We all enjoyed your devotionals from orbit."

"Don't know how astronauts lived without social media." The audience joined Jana in laughter.

"What are you doing now to spread the gospel?"

"Lots of public speaking in the past couple of years, teaching and testimony. And I have a new ministry, a therapy ranch outside of Clovis called Del Redentor, not far from where I grew up," The screen behind Jana showed images of the ranch under construction. "We'll use the lessons of Jesus and the beauty of horses to heal."

Baxter admired the images. "Looks like quite a spread."

"Well, it's not as big as your ranch, Baxter," Jana said, triggering another round of laughter. "But only the best for our Lord and Savior. We're getting a major grant from Iconium Industries to finish the facilities and pay for the first year of services." The audience applauded.

"Thank you, Jana," Baxter said. "Now we go live to Church of the Living Waters Jakarta, a satellite of our home church. Wait till you hear this worship team from the heart of the Indonesian mission field."

The stage manager signaled the end of broadcast. Baxter and Jana rose from their chairs and unclipped their mics. Members of the audience came to the stage apron to request autographs and selfies. Julius eased into the gathering, keeping watch on the throng pressing toward Baxter and Jana. Elijah slowly made his way forward. Baxter spotted him and waved him to the stage.

"Jana, this is Elijah Lindstrom, our newest hire," Baxter said. "A powerful engineering mind, he's teaching at the academy. Elijah, wouldn't Commander McAlister make a great judge for the robotics competition?"

"Incredible," Elijah said. Jana shook his hand, able to look him in the eye atop her western boots. "I was a member of your Out of This World Science Club in the seventh grade."

"I feel so old!" Jana brought her hands to her face in mock horror.

"I used the program later when I taught at camp. I owe you a lot."

Carla motioned to Elijah from the far side of the auditorium. Elijah excused himself. Jana walked Baxter to a corner of the stage.

"TV interview, robotics judge. What happened to 'bringing me in under the radar?'

"Couldn't resist using your star power. Brimstone 1 is top priority, but we still have our duty to evangelize and educate," Baxter said.

As the audience churned and chatted, Brad stayed in his seat, adding to the social media reports on the prayer vigil. A private chat app popped open on his screen.

"The astronaut has landed," Brad typed.

"We should meet," came the response.

"Where are you?"

"Closer than you know."

Hours later, Brad wrestled his Subaru Crosstrek down a dirt road miles from the ranch. The rocks and the wind made holding a straight path impossible. Instructions had stipulated parking lights only on the harrowing drive. Brad put his trust in the green line snaking through a GPS map of nothingness to reach his destination. The Glock 17 under his seat reassured him further.

A jagged silhouette rose against the stars. The map reported the shrinking distance to his end point, a rusted chain link fence finally confirming a manmade presence. Once he was past the fence, a new message told Brad to stop and get out of his car. He zipped his jacket against the wind's rhythmic blasts. A chorus of whistles and moans tagged each gust. Tumbleweeds spun out of the blackness.

Land of Enchantment, like hell, Brad thought as he plodded the broken ground and ducked the flying brambles. Another text came through:

TATE: 10 more steps.

Brad counted them off.

"Thought you'd never get here." Tate's voice came through the blackness. He activated a pistol-grip lantern. He was a few years older than Brad, dressed for Silicon Valley in hoodie and jeans.

"And where is here?" Brad shivered. He hoped Tate would blame the wind.

With sweeps of his spotlight, Tate revealed spindly steel towers, sloping conveyor belts hundreds of feet long, and broken catwalks. The surrounding metal maze startled Brad. The wind blew hard again. The whistling and pedal tones came from the air finding tunnels and tubes lacing the ruins, a ten-story pipe organ in the desert. Tate tugged Brad toward a large earthen berm.

"We're into commercial real estate big time," Tate said with a grand sweep of his hand. "Abandoned potash mine ... picked it up cheap."

"Abandoned?"

"Tunneling hit a natural gas pocket. Too dangerous to work. Prices for potash and gas too low to warrant fixing it."

"Sounds great." Brad couldn't hide the disdain in his voice.

Rectangular tunnels punctured the berm's far side. A gleam escaped the center opening. Tate led Brad into the welcomed illumination and windbreak. A hundred feet down, a small crew worked on a string of flatbed cars from the defunct mining operation. A bank of 3D printers extruded bearings and other axle parts, which the crew installed to refurbish the rolling stock. Several pickup trucks lined a tunnel wall, and additional workers augmented them with plates salvaged from mine scrap. Florid graffiti covered the wall behind the trucks. Spray-painted slogans and image—

many obscene—trailed down the tunnel. The most direct—The Humanist League Strikes! and Unrisen—left no doubt about the group's mission.

"We've been here about a year," Tate said. "We hike in over the trail system with bits and pieces. Occasional heavy drone lifts. I keep car traffic to a minimum."

Tate motioned his lieutenant Anik to join them. Three bodyguards came alongside as Tate and Anik took Brad deeper.

"Hydroponics and living quarters on the level below us. Fuel cells below that," Anik told Brad.

"Supplied by that natural gas everyone was so worried about," Tate added.

Brad surveyed the underground metal shop, astonished. "Looks like revenue's up."

"Never better," Tate said. "A new patron or two, plus the usual online enterprises."

"February 10 is a mission-critical date," Brad said.

"McAlister is onsite, but Brimstone 1 isn't even out of the box yet," Tate said.

"It's not about Brimstone itself. It's about The Package. It involves a radio transmission," Brad explained.

"The Package," Tate said. "Still no concrete proof?"

Brad shook his head. "I know this much. If anything screws up on February 10, Brimstone 1 stays in mothballs."

"Maybe we can explode Baxter's myth with software." Tate rapped his knuckles on a truck's completed armor. "The hardware solution will be messy." He pondered new moves. "We need to get Baxter off the ranch on that big day, disrupt him and his organization. Let's leak his ownership of all those interesting websites. Get me the domain ownership and hosting files."

"That's a huge breach." Brad grew alarmed. "They'll trace it back to me."

"Not if you're careful."

Anik held out a thumb drive to Brad. "Here's a program to help conceal your access to the files."

Brad ignored Anik. "I thought the plan was to take down Brimstone 1," he said. Welders hunched at a truck grill looked up at Brad's shrill echo. They resumed work with a look from Tate.

"The plan is to take down Christianity. Undermining Baxter Moore's leadership is one part. If we can ground Brimstone 1, that denies Moore any glorification in going to space. If we can't, we'll destroy the machine and everything onboard as planned," Tate replied.

"I can't do that kind of deep hacking. Julius and his team will tear me apart! Then you'll never stop Brimstone 1!" Brad said.

Tate held up his hands to calm Brad and led him into a side chamber. Anik did not follow. Once in the private area, Tate tilted his head and transfixed Brad with a sympathetic smile. The bodyguards grabbed Brad, gagged him, and pulled him deep into the chamber. Seconds later, they clamped Brad to an iron truss resembling a St. Andrew's Cross. The truss connected to a hoist, which Tate activated. His cries muffled, Brad ascended and swung over the chamber floor. The hoist stopped. Brad dangled above a wide, vertical borehole.

"Like I said, we're into commercial real estate big time," Tate said. "The property line is three thousand feet below you. Want to inspect it?"

Writhing in his restraints, Brad looked down the shaft. He screamed, head thrashing. League gossip had turned to prophesy. Body and time suspended, he reheard old whispers of how Tate made miscreants disappear. Brad arched backward, slamming his spine against the truss, attempting to defy gravity.

"Why hold back on Baxter Moore? Still trying to 'honor thy father?' Still being the accomplice?" Tate switched to a mocking tone. "'Honest, Mom, Dad told me he's pastoring in the next town. No, Mom, Dad isn't sleeping with the leader of the women's ministry ... with his secretary ... with a waitress he met this afternoon!'"

Tate walked to the edge of the borehole and peered into Brad's contorted face. "At least Daddy had the stones to chase real women. I wouldn't have found *him* creeping around a porn site."

Brad stopped writhing. He hung limply, his tears dropping three thousand feet. He surrendered to the pit.

"Three years ago, I gave you new messaging. I led you away from dirty little secrets and shame! And now you want to crawl back!" Tate retracted the hoist from the borehole and pushed a button to open the clamps. Brad crumpled to the chamber floor, heaving. Tate stood over him.

"If Brimstone 1 succeeds, they'll call it a Christian victory. Baxter Moore becomes a prophet and Jesus Christ gets a new lease on life. Your failure will strengthen the Christian lies and hypocrisy that destroyed your family." He whispered in Brad's ear. "I'd do anything to stop that. Wouldn't you?"

CHAPTER 3

Baxter picked up Jana at the VIP townhome complex on ranch grounds. The Moore corporate SUV plied a graded road and approached the ranch's horse barn, a recent minimalist construction with a copper roof and dark siding.

"Gorgeous." Jana stepped from the SUV, admiring the building.

"It was half of my daughter Belinda's birthday present," Baxter said.

"She must've loved it," Jana said.

"Once she got around to seeing it, six months after her birthday."

Inside, Baxter and Jana toured the stable row. The animals were purebred and immaculate, primarily quarter horses. A white head, narrow and chiseled with flaring nostrils, tossed among the darker, more docile equine profiles.

"Even more gorgeous." Jana reached toward the energetic horse. Muzzle strokes and soothing words calmed the animal.

"The second half of Belinda's birthday present," Baxter said. "This is Amyra, our Arabian. Her bloodline goes back to Leopard, a stallion the Sultan of Turkey gave President Grant."

"You're royalty," Jana said to the mare. With a signal from Baxter, a groom opened the paddock. Jana put a halter on Amyra and led her out of the barn. She took the horse in a slow walk around a ring, bending down to remove any stones or branches in the animal's path. Baxter paced Jana outside the ring fence.

"Eighty years ago, this was a real ranch," Baxter said. "Ten thousand head of cattle."

"Your satellite dishes would spook the herd." Jana looked beyond the barn to a house on a hill, pristine with clapboard siding. "Was that here eighty years ago?"

Baxter nodded. "The original ranch house. End of World War II, my grandfather inherited the spread from his uncle. Grandpa went from scientist to rancher to radio station owner within a few months. Moores have always been restless."

"Anyone living there now?"

"My father," Baxter said. "Diagnosed with Alzheimer's. I converted the house into his personal care facility. I pray he's comfortable, at peace." He smiled as he watched Jana handle Amyra. "You have her acting like a Shetland pony."

"Lots of misconceptions about Arabians," Jana said. "They're smart and brave. Give them respect, and they respond in kind."

"Want to take her out?"

"Love to. Join us?"

Baxter shook his head. "Indonesian foreign minister is calling in forty-five minutes. Fallout from the new web channel. They want to be clear there's no discrimination against Christians in their country. Give our girl a good ride. She needs it."

After properly warming up Amyra, Jana took her on the ranch trails. The mare was surefooted and inquisitive, responding eagerly to Jana's commands. Horse and rider descended a ridge to a flat straightaway. Jana felt the huge muscles gather.

"If you want to, Amyra," she whispered.

The mare burst from her trot. Mach 2, Mach 20—Jana had hit these speeds, but nothing replaced being one with an exquisite horse in a gallop. Jana urged Amyra along the straightaway and over a rise. She reined back, praising the mare, and patting her neck. From high ground, Jana spotted activity in the distance—the flicker of drones, a solitary figure looking up at them.

Jana dismounted and reached for her mobile phone. She affixed a small zoom lens, the phone becoming an impromptu telescope. Jana recognized the tall, dark-haired figure as Elijah. She winced when he dove his lead drone to the ground. When the craft remained intact and he repeated the maneuver, Jana determined the action was intentional.

Jana flicked her screen for maximum zoom. She wanted a better look at the lead drone's hardened belly that was striking the Earth. She also got an enhanced view of Elijah. While intent on his tablet and drones, he glanced around as if looking for surveillance.

Being a bad boy?

Jana debated riding over, but her phone vibrated in her hands. Staff Sgt. Ashley Grey, USMC, was IMing on the app Zhing. Jana had met her the previous year at a church conference. The message was short:

Commander, We need your help!

Jana tapped back, promising she would call within the hour. She mounted the mare. Elijah and his mystery squadron would have to wait.

Elijah hadn't spotted Jana watching him from a hilltop. He anticipated helicopters and SUVs, not a lone woman on horseback. A new problem overshadowed his nervousness about ranch security. Data was not transferring clearly from his striker drone to the rest of the formation. He checked his equipment and confirmed proper operation. There was another possibility. Elijah opened an app that detected RFI, radio frequency interference. He held out his phone and pivoted his body, trying to read any radio source jamming the link between his drones. A spike soon materialized. Elijah summoned his drones into the quiver and hiked toward the disruption.

Rounding an outcropping, Elijah received visual confirmation of the interference. The tower for KNMR, the original Moore radio station, stood a half-mile away. From the road, the station had appeared nonfunctioning. The RFI detection app said otherwise. Elijah moved across the open ground with determined strides, bent on resolving this mystery quickly. As he looked for an opening in the forbidding wrought iron fence, he appraised the antennas. A large metal horn stood on a mast next to the main AM tower, its scooped aperture more like a radio telescope than a design for commercial broadcasting. Behind the building was another incongruent rig, an X-shaped turnstile antenna.

A gate was unlocked on the far side of the fence. Elijah found the studio's back door also open. Easing into the room, he stepped into the late 1940s. The room was crammed with radio transceivers, amplifiers, and other electronics, all tube-driven, museum-quality. The equipment was not on display. All were active. Elijah heard a soft hum from several pieces, meters lit with needles trembling.

The room contained ancient items of comfort. A six-pack of glass Coke bottles, long since drained and washed, rested in a cardboard caddy with a wire handle. Magazines splayed on a side table. Atop the pile was *Amazing Stories* from March 1945. On the cover, a female space explorer with toned abs and a metal bandeau prepared to throw a switch. A green humanoid with pointed ears watched haplessly from inside a glass cylinder.

"So you decided to trade my bomb shelter for the radio station." The old man startled Elijah. "Always in the last place you look for it." The old man squinted at the small electronic part in his hand. "Bottom of the saddlebag."

Elijah recognized his escort from the previous day. "The door was open. I— "

"Take it easy. I don't tell on you. You don't tell on me." The old man removed the faceplate on an amplifier. "Keeping this place going will drive you crazy. But it's amazing what you can find online. Original parts lost in someone's attic. Company in Ukraine still making good tubes."

"Looks like you're transmitting," Elijah said.

"Running some tests. Getting ready for February 10, in case we need backup." The old man frowned at Elijah's puzzled look. "We talked about this before. Why are you here?"

"I was hired to teach at the academy," Elijah said.

"Right." The old man was incredulous. "Our ministry is about to take off, pun intended, and you show up. Hand me those wire snips."

Elijah produced the snips from a nearby tool roll. After trimming insulation, the old man soldered leads to the replacement potentiometer he'd brought in.

"I'm fine with you being around. No way we could keep all the secrets all these years. I trust the Lord has sent you to help my family." The old man finished soldering and was ready to test the pot. "Now if you could pass the voltmeter."

Elijah gestured, "I got this." He opened a digital multimeter app on his phone and applied a wireless probe to the connections. The readout confirmed live current.

The old man smirked at Elijah's phone. "Want to see a real handheld? I have the original."

"Motorola DynaTAC?"

"Not that wimpy junk from the '80s." The old man opened a metal cabinet and withdrew a device the size of a loaf of bread with a silvered antenna and angled mouthpiece. "SCR-536, walkie-talkie. My dad brought 'em home. They didn't have cell towers at Trinity." He pointed to framed photos on the wall featuring a man in his mid-twenties during World War II. "There's Dad with his boss, Dr. Fermi. That was quite a night."

The final picture showed the old man's father in tears with a balding, middle-aged man giving him a paternal kiss on the cheek—Enrico Fermi, Nobel laureate, a leader of the Manhattan Project.

"July 16, 1945," Elijah said, understanding the significance of the event captured in the picture, the detonation of the first atomic bomb north of Alamogordo, New Mexico.

"A few months later, Dad turned down Dr. Fermi's invitation to join him at the University of Chicago." The old man handed Elijah the SCR-536 to examine. "Dad bought this place instead and started our first Christian radio station. He always said he'd seen two Ground Zeroes, the Trinity test site and the radio station, the room we're in, to be exact. This is where he launched our main ministry."

"Spreading the gospel to all points?" Elijah said.

"*All* points."

Elijah looked closely at the walkie-talkie's control panel and laughed. "I didn't think they had LED technology during World War II." He pointed at diodes artfully added to the device.

"I made a few modifications. Still way cooler than any cell phone. You can have it."

"I can't take this."

"I've got a ton of them." The old man threw open the cabinet to reveal a row of the vintage walkie-talkies. "Maybe I can call you sometime." The old man grew quiet. "I don't talk to too many people these days."

Elijah waved goodbye and jogged back to the secluded spot where he'd flown the drones. The old man returned the wave and walked to a ravine behind the studio. He mounted a Harley-Davidson FLSTC parked under a mesquite tree—obviously not all products from the 1980s warranted ridicule. He rumbled out of the ravine and turned onto one of the ranch's graded roads. Several minutes later, the old man pulled up at the Moore family ranch house. He wheeled the bike into a detached garage and jogged to the backdoor.

The ranch house interior was another shrine to the 1940s, with modern additions including monitors and security systems. The old man carefully reactivated cameras once he was out of the frame. He ignored the small elevator and took the stairs to the second floor.

"You were gone too long," Marta said. "I can't keep covering for you like this. You're going to get me fired!"

Baxter Moore II patted his caretaker on the shoulder. "I'm related to the CEO. I'll put in a good word for you."

Marta held a stack of packages, Baxter II's latest online purchases. He exchanged the boxes for his dusty leathers, which Marta stashed. Moments later, Baxter II was in his Alzheimer's patient jumpsuit. He got into bed and pulled the sheets up to his chin.

"How's this?" He let his head loll and eyes glaze.

Marta laughed as she handed him a pill and a cup of water. "Take this, or you really will look like that again."

As his special prescription dropped in his palm, Baxter II smiled at Marta. "I'll come clean with everyone soon. Thanks for letting me have a little fun first."

"Your son will be so excited," Marta said.

"Sure. He owns fifty-one percent of the company that makes this stuff." Baxter II jostled the pill before swallowing.

Jana paced as she took the video call from Ashley Grey on the guest house flat screen. Ashley was in fatigues, calling from a hospital room. A man was in a bed behind her, unconscious, the tubes running from his body indicating grave condition.

"My husband was hit with 9mm rounds, well within the vest's protection level." Ashley tried to suppress her sobs.

"And they penetrated?" Jana said.

"Penetrated! The vest shattered on impact," Ashley said. "The doctors say he might as well have been wearing a live hand grenade. Along with the bullets, he had hundreds of pieces of shrapnel in his body."

"Have you talked to his CO? Your congressman?"

"I'm getting the runaround so far. Meanwhile, I'm finding other cases, service members and law enforcement ripped apart when their vests failed. It all comes back to one thing—Iconium Industries."

"Major manufacturer of disruptive fiber." Jana's head dropped.

"Their new product, Shelet, was in Frank's vest and the others," Ashley said. "I watched the prayer vigil last night. You said they're donating to your therapy ranch."

"Multimillion-dollar grant."

"It's a wonderful cause, but Iconium is killing people. If Frank doesn't stop bleeding internally, he'll be next." Ashley's tears increased. "I know what we signed up for as Marines, but we deserve a fighting chance. Instead, we get bad gear that helps the enemy kill us!"

Hours later, Jana poured over information from Ashley—medical reports, accounts from others wounded and killed while wearing vests containing the Iconium product, social media exchanges about defective fiber. During her investigation, Baxter messaged that he was still tied up with the Indonesian government's objections to content on the new web channel. Baxter's preoccupation gave Jana the time to form a drastic but necessary conclusion about Iconium Industries. She called the company's CEO, Ed Richie, and got his voicemail.

"I'm withdrawing our grant application," Jana recorded.

Jana donned a headset and haptic gloves for a virtual reality tour of Del Redentor, the therapy ranch she was building. The program mounted her on an avatar of Lightning Too, her horse boarded at her parents' property in Clovis. She had taken this cybernetic ride many times.

As Jana had said during her televised interview, Del Redentor represented the best for the Lord and Savior. The ranchland spread before her in faithful reproduction. Numerous trails wound from the main complex. She stopped at a barn and looked inside, each stall wired with smart technology to track horses' comfort and health.

She turned Lightning Too's avatar away from the barn and rode past the many arenas, ranging from small rings to competition-size spaces. The main arena stood in the distance, a grand indoor facility, climate controlled to negate the extremes of New Mexico's summers and winters. Jana toggled a control that superimposed a view of completed construction in the virtual landscape, an instant reckoning of the ranch's progress.

Jana reined toward a new trail. To the left was the equine hospital designed by her father, a retired large-animal veterinarian. On the hill before her was a beautiful sanctuary, the centerpiece of Del Redentor. She rode toward the church and heard another horse behind her.

"Feeling good, Commander. God bless you," a female voice called out. Jana knew wearable technology monitored by ranch therapists would verify the rider's positive announcement and prompt intervention if biometrics deteriorated.

"God bless you," Jana replied over her shoulder.

The riders stopped at hitching rails outside the ranch church. Jana tied off her virtual version of Lightning Too and walked around the horse to see who had joined her on the hilltop. The other equestrian was Lt. Rachel Thomas of Carrier Air Wing Eleven, Jana's former unit. Jana froze as she regarded the woman's avatar. Rachel had overdosed ten years prior, traumatized by an unprosecuted rape. In real life, she would never see Del Redentor.

Jana pulled off her VR gear, resolute. While compelled to refuse money from Iconium Industries, she would stop nothing, cut nothing at the ranch. She mulled current and prospective donors to email over the next few days and resolved to hit fundraising hard after completing her duties on Brimstone 1. Jana opened her US Naval Aviators Bible to a bookmarked verse:

> This is my command-be strong and courageous! Do not be afraid or discouraged. For the LORD your God is with you wherever you go. (Joshua 1:9).

Tears came to Jana, not out of fear but gratitude for the pending ministry. One more mission and she would go home to heal others. Her inbox flashed an alert from Elijah using his new Jeshimon Academy handle, a formal email addressing her as Commander McAlister. Elijah inquired about Jana's availability to discuss the robotics competition. He attached event guidelines and drafts of the student teams' engineering notebooks.

Jana sent a short reply, "Call me Jana. Zhing me." A few moments later, Elijah and Jana were connecting on the messaging app. Jana sent a link about a system designed for monitoring and judging robotics competitions.

> **JANA:** Have you checked out this new competition analyzer? Wireless. Reads and displays commands sent to robots and system responses. Works with smart tiles that snap together to create the competition floor. Provides better data for judging.
>
> **ELIJAH:** Looks great. The school doesn't have anything like that.
>
> **JANA:** Pick a configuration that would be good for this competition and future events. Send me the link and I'll buy it. Consider it a donation to the academy.
>
> **ELIJAH**: You being a judge is enough of a gift.
>
> **JANA:** I agree volunteering is the heart of a good cause. But sometimes, cash makes a big difference.

Elijah began examining variations and specs for the competition analyzer. His tablet chimed with an incoming message. He thought for a split second Jana was adding some thoughts on Zhing. Instead, the message came from the Moore Ranch Mysteries app. A community member was pinging Elijah's alias JustCurious regarding his "11 minutes" comment on ranch security response time.

ToldYaSo: Any more run-ins with Moore security?

JustCurious: No comment.

ToldYaSo: That's not helpful. We're supposed to support each other. Don't you want to expose the Moore family as liars?

JustCurious: Not interested.

ToldYaSo: Really? You know better than anyone Baxter Moore isn't looking for oil.

The comment jarred Elijah. He clicked out of the app and returned to the robotics website to select equipment for Jana to purchase. A banner ad flashed at the top of the webpage, promoting a manufacturer. Elijah ignored the clickbait as he concentrated on system specs listed below. The flashing became brighter and more persistent. Elijah glanced at the top of the webpage. The advertiser's images and copy had disappeared from the banner space. New copy sought Elijah's attention:

What is Baxter Moore REALLY doing on his ranch?
Check out Rig Alpha. What is he building?

Elijah caught his breath and refreshed the page. Another message filled the banner space:

Stop the lies! Stop Baxter Moore!
Join The Humanist League!

Elijah realized he was being hacked. He cleared his cache to delete any cookies tracking him and started a malware diagnostic on his tablet. Elijah chastised himself. Hanging out in dark digital corners meant contact with strange people.

Tate grunted as Elijah erased the sophisticated cookie he'd slipped onto his tablet during their chat, still a good first try. Brad had provided information on his interesting friend, now a Moore employee. Tate wanted to lure Elijah as well, just as everyone stationed in the abandoned mine had tripped one of his algorithms in their web surfing and social media posts.

Elijah would be a tough target but a valuable recruit. Tate consoled himself with a fistful of tortilla chips off his nightstand. He was miles away from the mine in another "commercial real estate holding," a dilapidated motel with a doused neon sign and no other occupants. When he tired of the subterranean amenities of hydroponic greens and incinerator toilets, he came here. He perused his online dashboard. The careful theft from a cryptocurrency exchange was nearly complete—funds split and tracks covered with his North Korean clients. Donations to The Humanist League were higher for the month. Business was going well, but Tate was on edge. The unease drove him out of the mine to a familiar place on the web.

Tate logged into a popular social media site as a contractor, just as he'd first done ten years ago. He entered a restricted section of the site reading Welcome, Moderator. His page displayed his old recognition badges: Top Moderator, 2015, 2016. He'd needed income and a channel for his energy after his tech start-up imploded. The Humanist League currently consumed him and refilled his depleted bank accounts. Still, he craved this old assignment.

A warning said the work pending involved highly disturbing images. Tate clicked the acknowledgment button and accessed a queue of photos and videos. He viewed the content—graphic depictions of violence, torture, racism, sexual abuse. He tagged images not suitable for posting on the social media site while absorbing the horrors. His computer automatically downloaded certain files for leisurely viewing, selections based on AI analysis Tate had run on himself. Tate's breathing matched the rush of images. He clicked furiously to display or ban.

A knock on the door interrupted the frenzy. One of Tate's bodyguards entered slowly. Tate nodded, and the bodyguard ushered a young woman into the dank motel room. Tate closed his laptop and got off the bed to welcome his guest.

"Welcome to the Motel Apocalypse," Tate said, the nickname for his hideaway. "You're doing excellent work, Mary. You've earned a night out."

"Marissa," the young woman said. Skittish but submissive, she took Tate's extended hand. The bodyguard exited.

"Marissa, wanna see something cool?" Tate shut the door.

CHAPTER 4

Early the next morning, Jana took another call on the flat screen in her guest suite. She sat at a small desk, a laptop, tablet, and notes before her. Ed Richie, CEO of Iconium Industries, was at his California headquarters.

"I know you're concerned about the stories you've heard." Ed's manner was earnest, a learned response to a business bombshell. "Our people are investigating. But let me assure you, Shelet is a good product."

"They aren't 'stories,'" Jana said. "A Marine contacted me from her husband's hospital room. I've seen pictures and reports. Your fiber is failing catastrophically."

"We need to approach this carefully. There could be many factors," Ed said. "Mistakes in installation by the vest manufacturers, incorrect information about the ordnance involved, improper use or even sabotage by the wearer—"

"Sabotage? I suggest you drop that talking point."

"Jana, I want you to say hello to a new member of our team." Ed adjusted his webcam to focus on a man sitting across from him at a conference table. "I don't think he needs an introduction."

"Hello, Jake," Jana's tone was familiar. "How's life in the reserves?"

"Going well. I get to defend my country two ways, in uniform and with a great company like Iconium." Jake flashed a smile that Jana did not return.

"You know from serving with Captain Henley how he supports our fighting men and women. As much as you do, Jana," Ed said. "And he believes in Shelet."

"How many times did we have stand-downs with the F-35? How many times did they say the plane was no good? How many kills did you end up having?" Jake's charming smile appeared again.

"Did she really lead the secret raid on that nuclear facility, wipe out all those Russian fighter planes?" Ed asked. Jake shushed him with a laugh. Jana's mood darkened.

"As long as we're jumping from disruptive fiber to jets, how about the 737 MAX?" she said. "How many warnings did they get about the software? How long did Boeing drag their feet? How many people had to die from a bad product?"

"I want you to have that grant." Ed steered the conversation in another direction. "As a Christian, I believe in your ranch."

"And you want me to believe in your fiber and your company in return?"

"The gift's gone public. If you turn it down—"

Ed finished Jake's thought. "People will want to know why. You'll condemn Iconium before we have a chance to deal with this the right way."

"Come to San Diego," Jake said. "You can tour the factory. We can look over the engineering and testing together."

"I don't have time. I'm in the middle of a major project with Baxter Moore."

"You're hunkering down with Moore. You're already talking to the media." Ed's CEO cool was cracking. Jake touched him with a calming hand.

"Jana, I'm convinced Shelet is safe," Jake said. "Let me convince you."

Jana shook her head. "I'm late for church. A lot of people need prayers this morning."

Church of the Living Waters was next to the interstate outside Todos Santos, boasting its own off-ramp and congregants from a 100-mile radius. The campus stood on karst land, signature New Mexico erosion creating clefts and columns in the rock. The giant sanctuary was buff-colored concrete, bending and undulating like a sacred spring bursting from the crags. The Moore family had spent untold millions and earned a spot on lists of the world's most beautiful churches.

Elijah crossed the broad terraces rising toward the sanctuary. Shiloh waved him over to where her youth group was gathering before the service. She introduced him to the other teens as "the new science teacher and robot overlord."

"Is this your first time here?" Shiloh asked Elijah. He nodded. She gestured toward the sanctuary's swoops. "Isn't this architecture amazing? How can they get concrete to do that?"

"With the right design, you can keep anything in place," Elijah said.

"Tell that to my hair." Shiloh flicked an unruly lock.

Shiloh guided Elijah toward the bank of entry doors, and greeters soon engaged him. The welcome might have seemed less homespun had he known a facial recognition program identified him as a newcomer as he'd walked the terraces. A black Suburban rolled up the private driveway leading to the sanctuary. Baxter and Jana exited, escorted by Julius. Elijah watched them enter the sanctuary through a side door before he walked into the main lobby.

The sanctuary had seating capacity and audio-visual technology to rival the biggest secular venues in America. Artists from the Moore Music label took the stage. The worship leader called the congregation to their feet as the drummer counted off and the band played the first song.

Many congregants, particularly younger ones, poured into the pit area, clapping and jumping to the upbeat music. Shiloh urged Elijah to join her and the youth group in front of the stage. Elijah went along, satisfied with clapping while the teens moved with the spirit freely.

Baxter and Jana sat in the VIP section close to the stage. Julius approached Baxter and spoke into his ear. Baxter nodded and motioned to Jana that he was stepping out. He and Julius left the auditorium area.

The exuberant set ended, and the congregants exchanged greetings. Elijah waved to people near him. A hand fell on his shoulder and turned him around.

"Everyone is having more fun down here," Jana said.

Shiloh sought her teacher in the throng to give him an official greeting. She found him engaging Jana, both laughing. Shiloh decided there would be no competing for his attention against the astronaut. Elijah noticed her easing away and motioned her close.

"Keep your eye on this one," a smiling Elijah told Jana. "She says her team is the favorite to win."

As the congregation returned to their seats, Humberto Morales, the church's pastor, took the pulpit to deliver the message.

"We've all heard the expression, 'When God closes one door, he opens another.' But what about Matthew chapter 7, verse 7? 'Ask and it will be given to you; seek and you will find; knock and the door will be opened to you.' How many times should we knock? When you stop with the knuckles and start with the forehead, that may be telling you something."

The congregation laughed, and Pastor Humberto continued his message about navigating boldness and foolishness, balancing disappointment with gratitude. He used examples from his family's journey to the United States, switching to Spanish to make several heartfelt points. At the end of his message, he invited the congregation to come forward for personal prayers. The band returned to the stage and played a quiet instrumental.

A line of prayer workers stood in front of the stage, praying with people one-on-one. Elijah waited in the short procession to talk to the pastor. When it was his turn, he whispered, "My forehead hurts. Make it stop."

Pastor Humberto smiled and put his arms around Elijah, praying that he accept God's plans for him, that he find gratitude and fulfillment behind his unexpected door. The pair shook hands. Elijah glanced down the line of prayer workers and saw Jana close to tears, finishing her personal prayer. Jana looked up and caught Elijah's eye. She managed a smile and gave him a quick wave goodbye.

That afternoon, Elijah was in his classroom at Jeshimon Academy, preparing for his teaching start. He hung posters produced on the school's large-format printer:

To one who has faith, no explanation is necessary.
To one without faith, no explanation is possible,
Thomas Aquinas.

Miracles do not, in fact, break the laws of nature,
C.S. Lewis.

God created everything by number,
weight and measure,
Sir Isaac Newton.

Brad entered the classroom, covering social media for the school. He aimed a digital camera at Elijah and began shooting.

"Look scientific." Brad clicked a series of photos. "When parents read the posts introducing you, they'll know their kids are in good hands."

Elijah cracked a smile as he continued his work preparing the classroom. To maintain candid pictures, he didn't look at Brad. "Got a weird contact online last night," Elijah said. "Guy seemed to know a lot about me."

"Where did he come from?" Brad moved around the room, grabbing more shots.

"Moore Ranch Mysteries app."

"Tsk, tsk, you don't belong there," Brad said. "You're part of the family now."

"He said I should know better than anyone that Baxter Moore isn't really looking for oil." Elijah stopped his classroom prep and looked toward Brad.

"Sounds like he read your report." Brad lowered his camera and tried to kindle a mutual laugh with Elijah. "Lots of crazy stuff out there about the Moores."

Brad started moving and shooting again. Again, Elijah stopped his routine and looked at Brad, who lowered his camera.

"I'm just the digital media guy. You're a substitute teacher as of forty-eight hours ago. Wanna binge on conspiracy theories about Baxter Moore, his dad, and his grandfather? There are tons of sites." Brad took the camera strap off his neck. "I like my job. I hope you'll like yours." He packed and left quietly as Elijah resumed working on his classroom.

At dusk, Brad drove to the motel. Tate stepped out of his room and walked toward Brad's car parked on the cracked asphalt lot. Brad handed Tate a thumb drive.

"That was fast," Tate said, gazing at the stolen data in his palm. "We're hacking Moore's law firm soon. We'll make enough of a mess to give you cover for extracting these files close to home."

Brad stood before Tate, silent. "Do you need a thank you?" Tate said.

"I want you to leave Elijah alone," Brad said. "He's not part of this."

"He'd be a great addition. Why don't you want him with us?"

"I don't want him to be a casualty."

Tate scoffed. "Says the near-casualty. We're at war. Elijah's best defense is to be on the winning side. I'm giving your friend a chance to come over. Just like I gave you." Tate handed Brad a keycard. "You're still upset from your time at the mine. You'll find the motel is nicer. That keycard will get you through the fence and into room 7. Good place to chill."

Tate nodded toward Marissa as she came out of his room. "Your sisters in the League are fierce. The best of them get to visit here too." Brad returned to his car, Tate's laughter trailing him.

By early evening, Elijah was back in his apartment under the school gym. He cooked his favorite, breakfast-for-dinner, on the small stove. He flipped eggs and continued surfing on his tablet. Brad was right. There were libraries of content decrying the Moores and speculating on their activities:

Baxter is plotting with the President to stage a fascist coup in America.

The Roswell flying saucer actually landed at the ranch in 1947, where a colony of aliens is now living.

There is no oil exploration. Baxter is a secret Satanist digging a tunnel to unleash the devil on Earth.

Baxter is building a rocket to release a bioweapon as a modern biblical plague.

Elijah looked at the SCR-536 walkie-talkie Baxter II had given him, set on the corner of on his desk. He'd first pondered whether the old man was a lunatic impersonator of the son of the original Baxter Moore, or if he was the real person, somehow in remission from the late-stage Alzheimer's described in his bio on the Moore Media website. The latter scenario became plausible given the old man's ease in traversing the ranch, the depth of his knowledge, the sincerity in his hope that Elijah was helping the Moore family. Elijah wanted to contact Baxter II to ask about the ranch oil project and the man's own cryptic remarks. He canceled the thought and stashed the conspicuous gift in a desk drawer, deciding to keep the vow of silence Baxter II had invoked.

Elijah heard an email chime. The communication was from a sales rep at the robotics site, responding to Elijah's request for a price on the competition analyzer he'd configured. The rep's quote was $16,590. She explained she was working Sundays to maintain her top sales ranking at the company. Elijah piled skillet contents onto a plate and opened Zhing. He forwarded the quote attachment to Jana, who responded a few minutes later.

JANA: Good job. I'll order it soon.

ELIJAH: Will you be here when it's delivered?

JANA: For sure. I'll even help you set it up. I'm doing a project with Mr. Moore, so I'll be around for a while.

ELIJAH: What kind of project?

JANA: Drone surveys of rock formations on the ranch.

ELIJAH: Really? I work with drones too.

Jana wanted to answer "I know" but decided not to reference her surreptitious viewing of Elijah on ranch property. She checked the time.

JANA: Speaking of the project, I have a meeting with Baxter in a few minutes. Promise you won't condemn me for working on the Sabbath.

ELIJAH: You have plenty of company. I was setting up my classroom earlier. The rep who sent me the quote actually bragged about working today.

JANA: No wonder the world is falling apart. Have a good first day in class.

Jana exited the VIP townhome complex, ready to walk the few hundred yards to the main offices. She found Julius waiting in his Bronco outside her building.

"Hop in."

"It's not that far," Jana said.

Julius smiled, his offering palm over the passenger seat. Jana nodded her assent. As she climbed in, she noticed stenciling on the fender of Julius' vehicle: Who Dares Wins.

"One of my favorite mottos." Jana pointed toward the fender. "You're SAS?" she said, referring Special Air Service, the British army's special forces.

"Captain, retired." Julius put the Bronco in gear. "Served in Afghanistan, Iraq ... and elsewhere."

"Sounds like my résumé. You may have called me in for an airstrike."

Julius shook his head. "My team took care of things on the ground, quietly. Jets and bombs tend to be loud." He shared a smile with Jana.

The Bronco stopped at the office building. Julius walked Jana into the lobby and handed her off to a security officer for escort upstairs.

"Good luck, commander," Julius said.

Jana found Baxter waiting in the conference room. He offered Jana a seat and aimed a controller at the video wall.

"We have confirmation of The Package," Baxter said.

A series of video clips tiled the screen. Each showed a view of the moon's horizon, taken from the lunar surface. A tag along the bottom read Beresheet 2 images. Mare Crisium. 08-01-25. Classified.

"Bought camera time on the Israelis' new moon probe." Baxter enlarged the first clip to create an extreme closeup of the starscape above the wrinkled ridges ringing the plain.

"There," Baxter said. A blurry shape, at first gleaming then seemingly blacker than the cosmic vacuum behind it, eclipsed a band of stars as it transited the panorama. Baxter clicked each frame individually.

Jana was transfixed. "Object in low orbit," she determined. "Another lunar probe?"

"No other spacecraft were scheduled to pass that way," Baxter said. "Nothing from Earth, that is."

"This was scheduled?"

"My father received the message in 1985. Moon orbit to be used for deceleration. Year, day, time of arrival all announced forty years in advance."

Baxter played the other video clips. They showed the object—The Package—orbiting lower and slower, taking longer in each clip to cross the view angle.

"No other confirmations?" Jana asked. "No radar signatures."

"Radar won't pick it up. You have to be looking for it," Baxter said.

"And then?"

"Slow arc to a point between the moon and Earth. Then comes February 10."

"The radio transmission?"

"We send a signal to The Package that shows we're ready to receive it. No signal, and it continues into deep space, into oblivion. It's been entrusted to us, and only us."

Jana stood and took the controller from Baxter. She manipulated the videos, replaying, freezing, and enlarging the views.

"I told you this was a recovery mission," Baxter said. "Eighty years in the making. Christianity's greatest revelation since the resurrection."

"What is The Package?"

"Not entirely sure. We can make some guesses based on the time it took to get here, what we see in the videos."

Jana walked the room, glancing repeatedly at the video wall, apprehensive. Bemused, Baxter watched her.

"Did you think I was crazy when I proposed Brimstone 1?" Baxter said. "Why did you accept the mission?"

"Because I believed you. I believed your family's discoveries," Jana said. "Because I'm Christian."

"A believer indeed. Now you can believe our footage from the moon."

"I want to talk to some people at NASA—" Jana started.

"No! We've been over this. Grandpa didn't tell Eisenhower, Dad didn't tell Reagan, and I'm not notifying NASA, the Pentagon, or the White House. Keep the covenant."

Jana reflexively pulled her mobile phone out of her pocket, ready to call somebody, maybe anybody.

"A phone call. That'll fix everything. That's what Ed Richie thought when he yanked me out of service this morning," Baxter said. Jana looked at him, pained. "Ed's convinced we're putting together an exposé on him and his ballistic fiber. He was raving."

Baxter put a hand on Jana's shoulder. "It took guts to give back the Iconium grant, the kind of guts I need now."

"It was the right thing to do, just like it's right to tell the world what's happening," Jana said.

"We will, in the proper way, at the proper time. That's always been the plan."

Jana remained rigid, clenching her phone. She stole another look at the video wall. With the videos looping, The Package repeated its flutter over Mare Crisium, confounding and tantalizing.

Baxter stepped back. "By end-of-business tomorrow, my bank will approve a loan to finish your therapy ranch. On your ranch's opening day, I'll retire that loan with an unrestricted grant from the Baxter and Marjorie Moore Foundation." Jana lowered her head.

Baxter was ready to close. "I'll start an endowment to keep the place running. I'll line up some strong donors to top it off."

"And all I have to do—" Jana said.

"—is fulfill the contract you've already signed, right down to the last nondisclosure," Baxter said. "Complete the mission."

Jana took a cleansing breath. She returned the phone to her pocket.

CHAPTER 5

"What makes you angriest about Christianity?" Tate paced the enormous cavern known as the Hub, two levels below the long incline where the rolling stock was being hardened. The Hub's sheer walls were swirled where machines had last scoured the mineral-bearing rock. Multiple galleries branched off the space. Tate's voice ricocheted in the passages.

The members of The Humanist League sat in a circle at the Hub's center. Each held a device—a phone, tablet, or laptop. Their fingers chattered as they responded to Tate's statements and engaged each other; however, his was the only actual voice allowed in the gathering.

"The book of lies, the so-called Holy Bible, says we must forgive." Tate took a few steps around the circle and paused. "How else will we swallow the injustice, the hypocrisy, the insults to our intelligence? Turn off your mind and forgive!"

Two people seated together whispered. "No talking!" Tate yelled. "Use your screens. They connected us originally. They bring us to a world ready to end this 2,000-year-old scam."

Marissa glanced at him. She was under orders not to mention her night outside the mine, as were several other female League members in the circle who'd been previous "guests" at Motel Apocalypse. Unable to eat or sleep after Tate's image sharing, she wanted to talk to him, but he remained distant once underground. Denied that outlet, she longed for counsel about the wrenching rendezvous. But the forbidden disclosure would mean a trip to the borehole and perhaps not merely to dangle.

"You know my story. I was molested as a child, in the name of Jesus. My mother hit and burned me when I told her, in the name of Jesus," Tate said. "Remember what was done to you in that name. Think how the world would be different and better without that name. Forget nothing! Forgive nothing!"

The clacks and beeps intensified as the circle typed, their equivalent of amen. "The Catholic Church will collapse under the weight of coverups and lawsuits. Mainline Protestants will continue to wither, too apathetic to even wring their hands," Tate pronounced. "But the evangelicals are dug in. They use the word 'war' like we do."

Tate stood on a boulder in the middle of the circle. "Their most dangerous leader is in the next valley. He's not a brain-dead hick in a double-wide. He knows media. He knows tech. He's worth forty billion dollars. And he's spending that money to ensure the name of Jesus lasts forever!"

Tate crouched and played with dirt and pebbles on the boulder's crown. "One day, they'll bring kids to this place, kids who won't be at the mercy of monsters serving a fake god." The dirt slowly poured from his hand. "Their parents will be rational, educated, wired for the future. They'll come here to honor you for destroying Baxter Moore and his Christian device, Brimstone 1."

Standing once more, Tate raised his phone. "Are you ready? Give me a *Y* for yes!"

The Humanist League simultaneously jabbed the letter *Y* on their devices.

"Are you ready?"

The keystroke echoed again in the cavern.

Tate came off the boulder while the League members remained in the circle, continuing on their devices. Anik took him aside and presented a tablet display. Tate smiled as he scrolled the stolen files.

Minutes later, Tate was deep in a gallery, making a webcall from a trailer that had been a foreman's office. The person on the other end, Chief of Staff Krista Simon, was in a cloister too, a surveillance-proof booth inside the Hart Senate Office Building, Washington, DC.

"We have everything ... all the additional websites he controls, the holding companies he uses, ad revenue," Tate said. "There's something to enrage everybody, even the most diehard evangelical."

"One person won't be enraged: the senator," Krista said. "She'll be delighted to nail Baxter Moore. She'll demand a hearing."

"That's what I was hoping. I need you to schedule it for February 10."

"That may be tricky. Any particular reason?"

"Of course." Tate let the silence hang.

Krista laughed. As a mole for The Humanist League, she knew better than to press Tate on too many details. "You'll get your date. When do I get the files?"

"Right after we kick up some digital dust," Tate said.

Elijah woke for his first day of teaching at Jeshimon Academy. His heart still diverged from the duties ahead. Checking his in-box, he saw a devotional urging sincere efforts on the job, including a paraphrase translation of Ephesians 6:6 warning about "just getting by." He smiled as he dropped greens into his new blender. Perhaps God was scolding him with the daily devotional, but he needed the reminder.

Elijah exited the rear door of the gym and traversed the quad to the science building. Carla spotted him across the expanse.

"How do you like your commute?" Carla called out with a laugh. Elijah waved back.

He plunged into his classes. Biology was his weakest area, but he was teaching an intro course and the textbook publisher had provided ample teaching guides, as he'd told his parents. He improvised away from the lecture at midpoint, drawing on engineering as he showcased nanotechnology emulating muscles and nerves to drive miniature machines.

"When in doubt, study God, the master engineer," Elijah said. The class laughed in approval.

By the afternoon physics class, Elijah had reclaimed the old joy he'd encountered teaching summer science camp. In examining thermodynamics, he took students from inner to outer space. Revisiting the earlier theme of nanotech, Elijah introduced them to particles that mysteriously disobeyed the second of the three laws of thermodynamics. He ended with descriptions of rockets and orbital craft that performed within the laws, by survival margins of millimeters and milliseconds.

After the bell rang and the students filed out, Shiloh approached Elijah. "More on the subject of overheating, Mr. Lindstrom, we revised the programming on our robot," she said. "Met the same workload with twelve percent reduction in system demand. She's running cool now."

"Excellent. Make sure to update your engineering notebook," Elijah said. "Commander McAlister will want to see what you learned leading up to the competition." Shiloh left the classroom with a smile.

Elijah started packing his gear. He glanced at the images still being projected. Per his discussion of rockets, a photo of a private space lift company's launch pad in New Zealand shined on the smart board. He had picked it because he liked the design of the service structure, the tower supporting the rocket on the pad. A company in California was marketing the structure to the burgeoning private space industry. A unique base bent like an upside-down wishbone into two steel curves anchoring the assembly.

Elijah cursed his deep memory and inability to set aside the Moore oil project. The chat room remark about Rig Alpha, made under Tate's pseudonym, also gnawed at him. Elijah opened a global mapping app and entered coordinates for the Moore oil exploration field. He hadn't viewed the satellite images for more than two weeks.

The shot of Rig Alpha was not pristine and did not benefit from supplemental ground-level pictures to enhance the image. But by zooming in on the object and its shadow, Elijah could determine Rig Alpha was now unlike any oil drilling tower he had seen. The tower's bottom had spread into signature wishbone bends.

Minutes later, Elijah was in his apartment, reconfiguring his spare drone, one of the Doves that chased the striker drone and took its readings. The redesign allowed him to remove the data transmission pack and install a digital camera with a stout lens. The new cargo would disturb the craft's finely tuned balance, but Elijah knew the drone would fly well enough.

As he was making final adjustments, Carla texted him:

> **Carla:** I didn't see you in your classroom after the bell. I want to know all about your first day.

> **Elijah:** It was great. Not to be rude, but I have to deal with a personal matter. Can we talk this evening?

> **Carla:** I'd love to. I know we threw you into everything really fast. Take care of your business. Text me later.

> **Elijah:** Will do.

Elijah checked the time. He still had enough daylight for some good shots. He quickly swapped his sport coat and loafers for a denim jacket and hiking boots. Soon he was driving toward the Moore Ranch.

Elijah picked a remote spot at the ranch's perimeter that would afford the shortest flight to cover Rig Alpha. After making final adjustments, he set his drone gently on the ground, lowered his first-person-view goggles, and opened the controller app on his phone. Elijah saw what the drone saw as he commanded take off. A slow ascent over the immediate hills led to the desired view, the Moore fracking installation, miles distant but discernible with the big lens Elijah had added.

Elijah focused on the drilling rig. Covered with work lights and scaffolds, the structure was taller than seen in the already dated satellite photo from the global mapping app, with extensions added. Elijah craned his neck for a better view and the drone at 1,000 feet mimicked his movement. The wishbone base now supported metal crossmembers similar to the pattern of the New Zealand launch pad structure.

Elijah nudged the drone farther into ranch territory, the lens straining to capture more detail. Suddenly the image of the rig disappeared. A hovering whirling mass filled Elijah's goggle view. He recoiled. His drone mimicked his motion. Adjusting his camera, Elijah captured a clear shot of what had come upon his machine—another drone, far larger, designed for power and payload. A primeval standoff in midair unfolded with the hulking predator slowly inspecting its tiny, astonished prey.

Elijah dove from his stationary position. The big drone overtook Elijah's drone and blocked its path. Elijah weaved but the pilot of the big drone anticipated his moves. The camera and lens destabilized his craft as anticipated. In frustration, Elijah throttled toward his pursuer, hoping mutual destruction might motivate the other pilot to veer off. The big drone evaded the suicide run.

The drones descended as Elijah pressed the attack. Finally, the big drone paralleled Elijah's machine and brought a stubby wing under one of Elijah's propeller guards. A flick of the wing flipped the little drone over. Control lost, the aircraft fluttered to the desert floor. Breathing heavily, Elijah tore off his goggles, not wanting to virtually experience the death spiral. He sprinted over a rise to where the craft went down.

From his vantage, Elijah spotted Jana studying the crumpled drone. "During World War II, Spitfire pilots would topple V-1 buzzbombs with that move. One of the earliest ways to kill a drone," she said.

"Thanks for the history lesson." Elijah scooped the wreckage.

"You were in restricted airspace."

"Why didn't you shoot me down with your F-35?"

"I tried to get you to leave nicely."

Elijah was eager to change the subject from his aerial embarrassment. "What's with that drilling rig? It's doubled in size. It doesn't look like any rig I've ever seen!"

Jana thumbed her phone. Elijah's phone played a cash-register sound effect from Zhing. Jana had sent him $3,000.

"Sorry about the damages," Jana said.

"Teach me those aerobatics and we can call it even," Elijah said as he calmed.

"Join the navy." Jana chuckled. "Earn your wings."

Jana turned toward her dualie parked on a dirt road, the big drone resting alongside. Elijah wanted to go after her, but he knew he wouldn't get any answers about what he just saw. He trudged back to his truck and tossed the remains of his drone in his truck bed. Slumping into the driver's seat, he hated depositing the money from Jana—the lady two decades his senior was patting him on the head—but his yawning bank account trumped his pride. The daily devotional rang in his heart again. Time to act like a teacher and report to the head-of-school about his first day.

Behind her own steering wheel, out of Elijah's sight, Jana hoped he wouldn't take the drone dogfight too hard. She had been flying her craft for pleasure, not to police the ranch. Still, the less Elijah knew about Brimstone 1, the better. The more she knew, the more she worried. Baxter's secrets outstripped those of any military mission she'd led. But she was stuck, her dreams tied with Baxter's. With the drone outing failed as relaxation, only one fix was left.

BRIMSTONE 1

A luxurious gym stood in the center of the living quarters complex on the Moore Ranch. Julius took a break from an early evening workout at the juice bar. He spoke on a video call to Brixton, his old neighborhood in South London. It was after midnight Greenwich time. A group of young adults huddled around the phone held by their pastor.

In the ring of faces, Julius saw himself long ago, coming into adulthood under his grandmother's care. She had arrived as a girl on the *Empress Windrush* from Jamaica in 1948, part of the early Black African-Caribbean emigration to England. At the end of the twentieth century, Julius's grandmother steered him from street gangs to the British army. "At least you'll get a medal for killing someone, not jail," she'd told him with her typical raw humor.

"We'll make you proud, Cap," one of the young women said. She and her group mates toted wagons and backpacks stuffed with food, water, socks, and scarves. They were ready to walk the hard streets of Brixton, giving out essentials—including God's grace—to the homeless.

"I'm already proud. Make our Lord and Savior proud," Julius said.

"It's cold, dark, and scary out here," said a young man.

Julius scoffed. "Have I told you about the time my patrol was trapped in an avalanche, twenty klicks from the Khyber Pass?" The group groaned and rolled their eyes. "Well, if you don't want to hear that war story again, move out!"

The young adults laughed, waved goodbye, and headed into the night. The pastor stayed behind to finish the call.

"You haven't been home for a long time. When do we get a visit, cousin?"

"I'm finally taking a few days leave. Staying local," Julius said. "Not sure when I can get a long holiday."

"Didn't get enough desert in Iraq and Afghanistan. Now you're in New Mexico. Fancy yourself Lawrence of Arabia?" the pastor said.

"John the Baptist." Julius shared a laugh with the pastor. "I've got my wilderness. You've got yours. Off you go."

As Julius ended the call, dull thumps sounded in the next room. Julius entered to see Jana in workout attire slamming a heavy bag with side kicks. She took a deep breath and started jabbing.

"Commander, I understand you ... intercepted ... Elijah Lindstrom on ranch property today," Julius said.

Jana looked at Julius from around the bag. Nobody liked being under surveillance, not even a retired military officer who grasped a clandestine project's security needs. She went back to her jabs. Julius leaned into the bag on the opposite side from Jana, allowing her harder punches.

"A little drone mishap," Jana said between strikes. "All better now."

"We're aware of Mr. Lindstrom's movements. You can leave him to my team with complete confidence."

Jana delivered a hammer punch. "Understood, Captain."

Jana stepped back, and Julius nodded graciously. Exploding from a fighting stance, he rocked the heavy bag with a roundhouse kick. Jana nodded in return.

In his apartment, Elijah had finished the check-in call with Carla. She'd already received positive reports from his students. In particular, the biology class had liked the nanotech machines that copied the workings of living organisms, God's designs.

Elijah retrieved video his drone had captured before Jana scored her kill. He juxtaposed a still of Rig Alpha with the image from his lecture. The comparison confirmed what he'd ascertained in the field: Baxter was erecting a tower identical to the service structure on the New Zealand rocket company's launchpad. Elijah perused the website of the service structure manufacturer in California but found no mention of any Moore enterprise as a customer.

The dawning realization shrank Elijah. He had called out a revered Christian tycoon about drilling for oil, oblivious to what was occurring. Did Baxter give him the teaching job out of pity? Was he laughing at him? Was Jana laughing at him? What part of "world-famous astronaut" did Elijah not understand? Had his childhood friend Brad knowingly placed him in this situation? That could explain why things had become strange when he'd talked to Brad in the classroom about the veracity of Moore oil exploration.

Elijah needed the teaching job. Quitting on Baxter Moore after one day's work would compound his messy separation from Colton Engineering in Williston. Unveiling more detective work about the realities of Rig Alpha could get him fired. Powerful people were lying and obscuring, and Elijah was trapped in the machination.

Elijah sank to his knees, digging elbows into his mattress, unashamedly praying like a scared boy at bedtime. "Lord, where have I put myself?"

After several minutes, Elijah reconsidered. He hadn't put himself anywhere. "You put me here, right?" Elijah did not receive an immediate answer, but he felt a calm. "I don't want to worry about anyone else's plans, God. Not even my own. Just yours."

In the middle of the night, the law firm of Parker, Stone and Kucera with offices in Albuquerque, Phoenix, Denver, and San Antonio experienced a massive hack, the digital equivalent of a tank driving through a storefront window for a robbery. The firm's chief information officer was on the phone with partner Roy Parker within minutes. The extent of compromise was unknown at this point.

"Do you want to notify clients?" the officer asked.

Roy Parker ran a rapid mental inventory of their highest priorities: the electric car manufacturer facing suits over vehicle fires, the country music superstar in his latest grueling divorce, Baxter Moore and his chronic secrecy in countless dealings.

"Not yet," Roy said.

Julius checked his digital security dashboard one last time. There were no red flags, no pressing issues thanks in part to Roy Parker's decision to keep the hack quiet. Nothing would stop Julius from enjoying three days off. He locked the front door of his personal townhome on ranch grounds, duffle bag over his shoulder, squinting toward the morning sun. A marked Ford Explorer from the local sheriff's department waited at the curb. Julius climbed into the passenger seat.

"Am I a wanted man?" Julius said.

"Definitely." Sgt. Wanda Benton leaned between the mounted laptop and long guns to give Julius a lingering kiss. Coming off her shift, Wanda had planned a packed three days—a stay at a beautiful inn on her tribal lands with mountain biking, music, and great food.

A yelp from the backseat interrupted the kiss. Julius turned to acknowledge Blue, Wanda's K-9 partner. Per standard law enforcement practice, the Belgian Malinois lived with Wanda and was traveling as well to the pet-friendly destination.

"Was I kissing your mummy?" Julius put his fingers between the bars separating the human and canine compartments. Blue sniffed them.

"Please, I'm her partner." Wanda put the cruiser in gear.

"She's 'Mummy' for the next seventy-two hours and we're one happy, off-duty family!" Julius said.

Across the ranch, another vehicle accessed the property. The delivery service driver knew the gate code at the driveway leading to the Moore family ranch house. The delivery truck climbed the drive and crossed the wooden bridge over the creek curving around the house, a dry gully in most months.

Watching the feed coming from the house's security cameras, Baxter II saw Marta receive the delivery at the front door. On his laptop, he checked the purchase off a wish list of electronics, motorcycle accessories, and music gear. An item from the latter category now held his attention, an intricately tooled leather strap for his Stratocaster. He checked his bank balance in a separate window—$18 million in a Swiss account, still plenty of "fun money" left. Baxter II put the $150 item in his digital shopping cart using his e-commerce alias "Jay Mann" and entered the original rural road address of the ranch house as the shipping destination.

Marta took the latest package to Baxter II,cscs cartridges of a new metal powder for his 3D printer. He was fashioning more parts for the radio station as an alternative to vintage finds on the open market. He tore open the sealed box. The powder composite promised better thermal properties in the finished pieces but required a firmware upgrade on his printer. Baxter II went to the basement and inserted the enclosed media into the machine, eager to load the powder and start his latest designs.

Returning to his apartment during lunch break, Elijah heard muffled beeping. He traced the sound to the desk drawer where he had stored the SCR-536 walkie-talkie. Baxter II was sending a Morse code message. The code key was another modification, a feature seen on kids' walkie-talkies of the '50s and '60s, not the units used by GIs in the '40s.

"Upgrading my 3D printer," Baxter II said in dots and dashes. "You should check it out."

"Most people text these days," Elijah tapped back methodically. His Morse code was rustier than his biology.

"Smiley emoji," Baxter II spelled out.

CHAPTER 6

Baxter sprawled across his bed in the latest Moore Ranch house, a high-tech hacienda near the townhome complex for VIPs and top staff. An electric bleating punctured his hard-won sleep. He grabbed his mobile phone.

"We've got a fifteen-minute heads-up." Tanya Cummings, Moore Media's lead anchor and news director continued, "*The Post* is naming you as the hidden owner of several of the most radical sites on the web ... alt-right, alt-left, all over the spectrum."

"Sit tight." Baxter rubbed his forehead. "Let's see what they've really got. My official response should come first from Moore corporate communications." A second caller appeared on his screen, attorney Roy Parker. Baxter switched to the call.

"Roy, if you're telling me we're in crisis mode, you're late," Baxter said.

"We got hacked in the middle of the night," Roy said. "We're still not sure what they got, if anything."

"So you wanted to cover your butt before you called me."

"Baxter, we get probes and attacks all the time. Usually we fend them off, and we don't have to worry our clients."

"Now this client ... or should I say soon-to-be former client ... is worried. I'll be dragged through the streets in a few minutes."

"About that. I just heard from our people in DC. Senator Fairchild is holding a news conference in an hour."

"An hour after the story breaks? How about an hour before?" Baxter left the bed. "My old friend on the Hill is slipping."

"And this old friend reminds you we still don't know where they got the information. Don't fire us yet. You'll need a good lawyer."

"You'll need to prove I've got one!" Baxter sent his phone flying.

Later that morning, Baxter monitored news on the media wall of his conference room. *The Post's* exposé stood as a text display at one corner, updated as the writers added details throughout the day. Julius entered without a knock, the only person in the Moore organization given such grace.

"Sorry for ruining your getaway," Baxter said. "Any leads yet?"

"I talked to Roy Parker's information security officer from the road," Julius said. "The hacker made a mess of things on their system. Very showy, I'd say."

"What's happening internally?"

"We've compiled a list of potential hackers within the Moore organization, people with sufficient access or skills. Twenty-nine names so far."

"That'll take forever to plow through."

Julius called up his list of suspects on a screen. "We're working as fast as we can. If it was an inside job, it was sophisticated and smooth, likely with high-level help from outside."

"The Humanist League," Baxter said. Julius nodded. "I'd love to think Fairchild is in league with them, pardon the expression." Baxter restarted the video window containing the senator's news conference.

"America has suffered enough from fake news, fake social media accounts, and online manipulation that puts us at each other's throats, that rips apart the fabric of our nation." Sen. Fairchild spoke from a podium inside the Hart Senate Office Building. "As we are learning this morning, Baxter Moore is not content with his empire of Christian and conservative media. He has built a shadow empire of radical fake news sites and inflammatory social media platforms on the internet. The 'official' owners of these sites and their hosting providers are a maze of shell companies. But everything leads back to Baxter Moore."

The view switched to a collage of screenshots from the various sites and pull quotes from *The Post* article. Sen. Fairchild continued, "We'd expect Baxter Moore to back vicious alt-right sites, and he does, based on what we're seeing. But he also owns an equivalent number of alt-left sites. Conspiracy theories, calls to violence, hate speech ... it's all there from across the ideological spectrum. It reminds me of Russian trolls pumping out conflicting propaganda a decade ago to confuse and frighten our country. Now we have a new secret troll factory. It's called Moore Media."

A closeup of Sen. Fairchild filled the screen. "Why, Mr. Moore? What's your agenda? What damage have you done to American hearts and minds? I intend to find out."

Donna announced an incoming call from Roy Parker. Baxter stopped the video of Sen. Fairchild's news conference and opened Roy's image on the media wall.

"Expect a request from Sen. Fairchild to appear before Congress," Roy said.

"When's the hearing scheduled?"

"February 10."

Baxter and Julius exchanged a look. "And if I say no?" Baxter said.

"You'll be subpoenaed."

"I could drag it out with court action."

"Let me stop you right there," Roy said. "The telecom bill is gathering steam. Fairchild is adding amendments. If it passes in current form, the federal government will be able to pick apart your business, every license under retroactive review, more stringent service area ownership rules, more vulnerability to lawsuits. It'll mean the end of Moore Media as we know it."

"So you think we'll get the votes to stop the bill if I cooperate?" Baxter said.

"It's our only chance," Roy said. "You take the hot seat. Otherwise you become the phantom menace of mass communication. You'll push the fence-sitters to the yea column."

Baxter ended the call. "Pulling me off the ranch on February 10. It would take a proverbial act of Congress." He messaged Brad to come to the conference room.

Brad knocked before entering, and then summoned all his willpower not to jump when he saw Julius seated with Baxter.

"What's the word on the street, as we used to say?" Baxter said.

Brad breathed in relief. Baxter sought a social media report and not an interrogation. Brad got behind the conference room keyboard and called up his dashboard that tracked online communication relevant to Baxter Moore and Moore Media.

"You're top-five in trending news this morning." Brad pointed to performance graphs on his dashboard. "Sentiment tracking at fifty-two percent against you, forty percent supportive, and the rest neutral. Among the forty percent, about six out of ten feel *The Post* and Sen. Fairchild are spreading fake news about you. The remainder want to learn more."

"Could we lose the support of the 'want-to-learn-more' group?" Baxter said.

"Yes. A lot of people are worried the sites are unchristian." Brad enlarged a stream of relevant posts compiled from multiple platforms, keywords highlighted, analytics below the stream measuring sentiment subcategories.

"I want hourly updates, please. Thank you, Brad," Baxter said.

"He's one of the possibilities." Julius brought up his list of suspects again after Brad left.

"What about Elijah?" Baxter said.

Julius highlighted Elijah's name on the list. "He is too, but his clearance level isn't nearly as high as Brad's. All the same, he's brilliant and a sneak. He's slipped onto the ranch a couple of times, flying those drones."

"Carla says his students love him," Baxter said.

"So he's doing a good job at the school. At least that's one thing we don't have to worry about," Julius said. "All the same, I want to stop his unauthorized visits. We need to tighten up in general."

"Don't scare him off," Baxter warned.

"If he runs, we'll know he's our man and we'll track him down. If he stays, he's more likely clean."

"Or very confident."

"Just remember, you pulled him to our bosom," Julius said.

Baxter began closing video screens on the wall. "I'll be heading back from DC during the transmission window. I'll direct everything from the air. Engineering will upgrade my jet's communication center. I want overkill on power and bandwidth."

Baxter stood, prompting Julius to his feet as well. "I want to move up the launch for Brimstone 1," Baxter said. "Eight days after we transmit, The Package enters Earth orbit. From that point, the longer we take, the stronger our enemies get."

"Better tell your astronaut," Julius said.

That morning, Jana ate breakfast in her guest house after a workout. She watched breaking news about the websites. A knock sounded on the door. Jana found an envelope on the step, the courier vanished. She shook her head at the Moore organization's stealth as she extracted a keycard and note from the envelope. The message directed her to a location on ranch grounds where she could further prepare for Brimstone 1.

Later that morning, Jana went to the Moore office building. Waved on by the lobby officer, she entered an elevator. A display screen above the elevator buttons read: "Keycard detected." A stainless-steel panel slid open beside the standard buttons, revealing another set. Jana pushed the lowest one and descended.

The elevator opened to a sub-basement corridor with a security door that unlocked with her card. Jana entered a room marked Library. The chamber upheld the Moores' penchant for time-arrested spaces, this one circa 1979 with dark wood paneling and furniture swathed in orange and brown fabrics. The tech was updated with a media wall similar to the one in Baxter's conference room across the widest vertical expanse.

A wireless keyboard, a controller, and a written note rested on a table facing the media wall. Jana read the new set of instructions:

> You now have complete access to project archives. Take your time and review. I'll answer any questions the best I can. Baxter.

At the master index Jana found an interactive timeline with files and recordings in chronological order from 1948 to the present. She selected the first file: Baxter Moore I, February 1948. A page appeared akin to an online encyclopedia, an audio module dominating the layout. Jana clicked play.

The recording began with Baxter Moore I, grandfather and father of the current Baxters:

> My name is Baxter Moore. It is February 1948 by the way we measure time on Earth. Before receiving this message, you may have seen bright flashes from our planet—atomic explosions, one test in New Mexico, two wartime uses in Japan, two more tests in the Pacific Ocean at Bikini Atoll. There will be many more such explosions, hopefully only tests. I helped develop the atomic bomb. I'm sorry. I'm especially sorry if earthlings destroy ourselves with these weapons before we can communicate or meet.

Images and hyperlinks scrolled beside the audio module, providing supporting information. Jana saw pictures of Baxter I at Los Alamos and the Trinity test site, similar to the framed photos in the radio station. The recording continued:

> But there is a power at work on Earth greater than nuclear weapons—God, creator of the universe. He made me and my people. He made you, if there's anyone out there to hear this. I think there is, and I pray your ways are closer to his than ours are. Yet, you may be unfamiliar with God the creator. He gave us his living Word to share his love and teachings. I will share it with you.

A promotional photo scrolled into view of Bing Crosby with Baxter I and his wife. The caption printed on the original glossy read: Bing Crosby presents Bax and Marge Moore, KNMR, Albuquerque, with revolutionary magnetic tape recording and playback system. Bing says, "For radio broadcasting, tape is the future!"

> The next voice belongs to Bing Crosby. If you've been listening to our planet's transmissions, you've heard a lot of this gentleman. He's not a head of state or clergy. He is an entertainer, perhaps the most famous person on Earth, and a friend. And now, The Holy Bible.

The historic baritone of Bing Crosby commenced narration, a tape recording that had been included with the system he gave the Moores, spliced onto Baxter's greeting:

> The Book of Genesis. In the beginning God created the heaven and the earth. And the earth was without form, and void; and darkness was upon the face of the deep. And the Spirit of God moved upon the face of the waters. And God said, Let there be light: and there was light.

Jana stopped the recording and returned to the timeline index. She skimmed milestones:

First response: June 1960
Baxter I mapping of communication origin: June 1960
Baxter I reply: July 1960
Baxter I video message to successors: August 1960
Second response; first acknowledgment of bilateral communication: April 1973
Baxter II demo tape: April 1973

A demo tape amid the other momentous files caught Jana's attention. She activated the audio recording. At age thirty, Baxter II tuned his Martin acoustic guitar and announced the title of a new song: "Why, Abba, Why?" He experimented with a verse, adjusting melody and lyrics.

Jana heard someone entering the room. Baxter stopped playing. "Hey, my man," he said.

"Daddy," said Baxter III, age six. "Why were you and Grandpa yelling at each other?"

Baxter II sighed. "Grandpa told me some things I hadn't heard before. I had a hard time believing him. I got upset."

"He's not really crazy, is he?"

"I didn't mean it. He's not crazy. Grandpa's a genius."

"Is he all right?"

"No. He's sick, very sick. That's why he wanted to have that special talk with me."

"Daddy, are you going to have that special talk with me?"

"Someday."

"OK. I promise I won't call you crazy."

Baxter II laughed.

"If I hadn't walked in on my dad that day—" Jana flinched as Baxter III entered the library, drawing her out of immersion in the archives. "Year after year, I kept asking about 'that special talk.' We finally had it when I was still young, maybe too young."

"And you didn't call him crazy," Jana said.

Baxter shook his head solemnly as he took over at the keyboard. He opened several files including "First Response: June 1960."

"My grandfather had set up the taping system Bing Crosby gave him, waiting to capture any transmission from where he'd aimed his Scripture broadcasts," Baxter said. "It was silent for twelve years. And then—"

Baxter played the First Response file. High pitches screeched. After a few moments, the sounds repeated a sequence. Baxter I slowed the tape. Jana heard a series of dots and dashes, Morse code in English. The letters seemed random, with few discernible words. Numbers interspersed with the other figures.

"That's the original frequency equation?" Jana said.

Baxter nodded and expanded a photo his grandfather had taken of a chalkboard. Scrawled across was the frequency equation Baxter I had deciphered from the first response.

"A code for hopping, same technique we used during World War II for guided munitions and encrypted communication," Baxter said. "My grandfather built a controller to hop the frequencies. He then received this, the first recording you heard when I approached you about Brimstone 1."

Baxter started another audio file. What seemed space noise, naturally produced radio waves, coalesced across the wider bandwidth created by the hopping. The stellar howl became a moan, which became a voice.

"Use transmission equation," the voice said. The pitch and cadence compressed and distended as the statement repeated.

"Do not announce. Punishment," the voice repeated three times. Baxter paused the recording.

"At the beginning, the sender asked us not to disclose the communication," he said.

"'Punishment.' That comes from laws, a social order," Jana said.

Baxter restarted the recording from space.

> Believe. "For the invisible things of him from the creation of the world are clearly seen, being understood by the things that are made, even his

> eternal power and Godhead; so that they are without excuse:" Romans, first chapter.

Baxter paused the recording. "My grandfather had alternated tapes of the Old and New Testament, foundations of the faith alongside the lessons of Jesus. He checked his log for when he'd first broadcast Romans."

"Calculating distance based on radio wave speed and time needed to receive and respond," Jana said.

Baxter opened the file of his grandfather's star charts, markings indicating where the messages had likely originated.

"No solar systems at origin point." Baxter complemented digitized versions of the 2D charts with a 3D animation of stars nearest Earth. The image highlighted a swath of space beyond Barnard's Star, a gulf between known solar systems. Jana rotated the image, looking back from the hypothesized origin point toward Sol, the Earth's sun.

"An object in interstellar space harboring intelligent life," Jana said. "A ship or space station. Could be a rogue planet or asteroid but without a star to orbit, it would need artificial systems to support life as we know it. Whatever the case, all beyond humankind's capabilities."

"Same conclusion reached in 1960," Baxter said. "We're not dealing with someone living easy who's simply equaled Marconi."

"Maybe it's a wayward angel," Jana mused.

"Then heaven is only a few light years away and they're handing out radio transceivers instead of golden harps." Baxter restarted the recording.

> Talk. "And he said unto him, If now I have found grace in thy sight, then shew me a sign that thou talkest with me." Judges, sixth chapter.

Baxter hit pause as it began to repeat.

"And we have talked, with a lag of twelve or thirteen years between every conversation. In secret," Baxter said.

"Grandpa followed the instruction. Besides, he didn't want to be branded a lunatic or fraud without physical evidence. Same with Dad, who then learned we'd have our evidence, but it would take decades. Just be patient—"

"And leave it to his son," Jana said.

Baxter sat in silence before responding. "Moore Media has been called 'the true global church.' People don't realize how far our reach goes. God didn't grant my family this favor, this power lightly. And you're right, everything has been left to me to finish. The Bible provides a warning."

"Are you thinking end times, book of Revelation?" Jana was uneasy about Baxter's sudden darkness.

Baxter shook his head. "Kings and Chronicles." He balled his fists. "I cannot be a failure in Solomon's footsteps."

Baxter stood abruptly, sending his wheeled chair scuttling across the linoleum. Jana rolled the chair back to the table and watched Baxter march into the corridor toward the elevator. She reviewed the star charts for a few more minutes before shutting down the media wall. By the time she returned to the Moore office building lobby, Baxter was gone. Her phone vibrated with a waiting message, reception having been lost while underground.

ELIJAH: The competition analyzer has arrived. Still want to help me set it up?

JANA: Nothing would please me more. See you in an hour?

ELIJAH: Yes, ma'am

The school day was over. Elijah and Jana were alone in the gym, paving a section of the court with the smart tiles that would comprise the robot competition arena.

"Interesting news today about the boss." Elijah connected a tile to one Jana had just placed.

"That's an understatement," Jana said. "He messaged me on my way over. Sen. Fairchild is calling him before Congress on February 10, and he asked me to go too."

"Are you going to speak?"

"No. I think Baxter would like allies in the hearing room."

"Sounds like your duties are expanding from drone surveys." Elijah's gaze remained on the tiles he was joining.

"You are into drones, aren't you?" Elijah looked up and found her eyes boring into his.

Elijah broke from the stare and hurried to the analyzer control station. He commanded a test robot onto the smart tiles. Readouts appeared on the large monitor connected to the control station. The system checked out. Elijah beamed with the activation and Jana clapped softly.

"This day needed something to celebrate," Jana said. "How about dinner for a job well done?" Elijah smiled and nodded as he began shutting down the equipment.

The Dunromin Travel Center outside Todos Santos had the area's highest restaurant ranking on review sites. Elijah and Jana came inside as rain started. The hostess recognized Jana and respectfully asked for a selfie. Jana and the hostess huddled for the picture.

"This will be great for our marketing," the hostess said as she posted the shot on social media with the caption:

Look who's dining at the Dunromin Travel Center. Astronaut Jana McAlister! @theRealCommanderJana #americanhero @dunrominTC #goodfood

Over iced tea and salads, Jana learned about Elijah's exodus from North Dakota and how he saw the teaching job as a stepping-stone to a higher position with the Moore organization.

"Do you ever see yourself going back to Williston?" Jana said as the server set down the main courses.

"Not likely." Elijah compressed his huge burger for a bite.

"Isn't there someone you might miss ... folks, buddies, girlfriend?" Jana said.

"Things are better with my dad long distance. My friend Brad Ferris also works for Mr. Moore, which is how I got here," Elijah said. "As for a girlfriend, that ended when I left Colton Engineering." Jana looked up from her dinner. "Her name is Colton too, as in Dave's niece."

"Talk about a breakup," Jana said.

A ringtone sounded on Jana's phone, a film noir motif. Already knowing the sender from the assigned tone, Jana read the incoming text and cursed under her breath.

"Elijah, I'm sorry, but could you excuse me for a few minutes?"

Jana exited the restaurant. Elijah picked at his food and checked his phone. He speculated that Baxter had called Jana away regarding the brewing website scandal.

The hostess approached the table. "Sir, I don't mean to intrude, but Commander McAlister is outside with some strange guy. They seem to know each other, but he's yelling. Maybe you want to see if she's all right."

Jana led her visitor into a secluded part of the parking lot as he was becoming more agitated. Jake Henley, the man alongside CEO Ed Richie on the Iconium call, was unconcerned about spectacle, a mood embellished by drinks before texting Jana he was outside the restaurant.

"You have to patch things up with Ed. You're making me look like a fool!" Rain and sweat coursed down Jake's face.

"You shouldn't have sold yourself as the Jana Whisperer."

"Once upon a time—" Jake said.

"It's over. Everything is over!" Jana said.

Jana turned to leave. Jake grabbed her arm and bent it behind her back. Jana pivoted in the direction of the twist to reduce its force and smashed her boot heel on Jake's instep. Jake let go and Jana completed her spin, ready to kick the knee now supporting all his weight. Jana was surprised when she saw Jake missing from her field of vision.

Elijah barreled into Jake a split second after Jana's heel strike. The men rolled before Jake pushed Elijah away. Both stood and squared off. At 6'5" Jake had two inches on Elijah.

He smiled, eager to give the younger man beating. The air cracked. Both men's heads jerked at the sound.

Jana had drawn a Springfield Armory XD Mod.2 from her small-of-back holster and fired a .45 bullet skyward. Jake relaxed his fighting stance and turned.

"Wasting a round on a warning shot, Jungle? I trained you better than that." Jake addressed Jana by her call sign.

"I'll only need one more." Jana aimed at Jake, center mass.

Vanquished, Jake shambled into the sheets of rain. Jana reholstered the pistol. Elijah was skinned from hitting the asphalt, his nose bleeding. Jana hustled him into a restaurant bathroom. She wetted paper towels and applied them where he bled.

"Are you all right?" Elijah asked.

"Yeah." Jana shook her head. Elijah was the one banged up.

"Who was that guy?"

"Someone from the past." Jana prepared more paper towels.

"Shouldn't we call the police?"

"No."

"I'm worried about you."

"I don't need anyone worrying about me," Jana snapped. "I don't need a hero."

"And I don't need a mommy." Elijah yanked the compress Jana was holding on his arm.

Jana threw the remaining paper towels into the sink and stormed from the bathroom. Elijah heard her ask the hostess for the check. He steadied himself against the counter and shut his eyes.

CHAPTER 7

"And when they say people from 'way out west' don't know tech?" Jana spoke from the speaker's platform in the gym. Alongside were pop-up displays chronicling her major achievements and evangelism, standard gear for her public appearances.

"I can do all things through Christ who strengthens me!" the audience replied from the bleachers.

"And when they say women can't fly in combat?"

"I can do all things through Christ who strengthens me!"

"And when they say you can't go into space?"

"I can do all things through Christ who strengthens me!"

Jana raised her hands to end the call-and-response. "'Slip the surly bonds of earth, put out your hand, and touch the face of God!'" she said, paraphrasing the poem "High Flight." Her speech concluded, the audience cheered. The contest analyzer smart tiles marked out the arena. The robotics competition was about to begin.

"First teams, you have ten minutes to get your robot demonstrations ready," Elijah announced. "Go!"

The student contestants dispersed, adjusting robot appendages, and checking command sequences on touchscreens. Jana and Elijah descended the platform.

"Sorry about the other night," Jana said. "Jake played tight end at Annapolis, and he was a pilot survival instructor. I didn't want you hurt."

"It would've been a noble death," Elijah said.

"Other than Jesus taking the cross, there's no such thing."

"Then I won't think of myself as a hero. I definitely don't think of you as my mother." Elijah smiled before walking away for final checks with the students.

Throughout the day the teams rotated through design inspection, performed their routines in the arena, and interviewed with the judges. Jana took the lead with the chief telecommunications engineer from Moore Media, Wally Hastings, and a retired science teacher from Jeshimon serving as associates. Elijah kept the competition on schedule, encouraging teams and providing slight assists within the rules. Once the rounds were finished, Elijah declared the competition phase over, and the judges went into a coach's office to tabulate scores and determine winners.

The gym fell silent once Jana returned with the results. She pointed at her heart. "In the 1990s, this New Mexico high school student saw robots move from science fiction to the factory floor and the surface of Mars. And I wanted to move with them. I can only imagine the breakthroughs you'll see ... and create. The hard work, creativity, and spirit of every team has been amazing, but as you know, there can only be one winner. The Excellence Award goes to Thy Kingdom Code!"

Shiloh and her team screamed. They ran to the bleachers to receive hugs from loved ones before crowding onto the speaker's platform. Carla presented the team members with their awards while Brad took pictures. The team posed for more shots on the arena floor clustered around their winning entry, the robotic home health care aide.

"So, Mr. Lindstrom, is it possible to be bold and humble at the same time?" Shiloh hoisted the first-place trophy she had predicted for her team.

"All part of squeezing through the narrow gate," Elijah said, referencing Matthew 7.

The competition ended, and contestants and audience dispersed. Elijah walked Jana to her truck, carrying her pop-up displays rolled back into their metal bases.

"I'm humiliated," Elijah said. The words came suddenly but softly, as if he were thinking aloud.

"Seriously, forget about the other night," Jana said.

"It's not that." Elijah lowered the displays into the pickup bed. He turned toward Jana. "Baxter Moore said he was looking for shale oil deposits on his ranch. That explained the construction, the activity. I came down here to set him straight."

"Don't beat yourself up for being brilliant."

"Am I so smart?"

"Smart enough to develop new technology ... to earn an audience with a billionaire ... to be the best teacher those students could ever hope for."

"Smart enough to get in the way of what you and Baxter are really doing?"

Jana paused. She wished she could tell Elijah many things. "I can't stop you from figuring stuff out. I'm thinking you can't help yourself."

"But this is above my pay grade."

"That line originated in the military. I've spent my life there, waist-deep in secrets." Jana put a hand on Elijah's shoulder. "Nothing stays hidden forever. Keep your eyes open."

Elijah lingered in the parking lot and watched Jana's dualie disappear on the road to the ranch. Brad approached him, carrying his own gear to his car.

"Looks like you're friends now." Brad nodded toward the departing truck. Elijah turned his back on Brad and returned to the gym, convinced his old "friend" was party to the oil exploration ruse.

That evening, as Elijah packed competition booths and gear, a knock echoed through the empty gym. Julius entered, smiling at a startled Elijah.

"Mr. Lindstrom, I'm Julius Dunbar, director of security for Mr. Moore." The announcement filled the vault. "I saw the lights on."

"Making your rounds?" Elijah returned to dismantling competition items.

"Not exactly. I'm here to see you."

"Sorry you missed the robotics competition." Elijah lifted a folding table onto a wheeled pallet. Julius crossed the court toward him.

"We hear it was a big success. We also hear you're an excellent substitute teacher."

"Thank you." Elijah pulled the pallet toward another table.

"Things are working out well for you. Respectable job, free room and board, connection with a very wealthy and powerful man."

"I know a blessing when I see one," Elijah hefted the next table.

"I'm sure you do. We need to steward our blessings."

"I promise to keep up the good work."

"You've received a lot of leeway, Mr. Lindstrom." Julius's voice took an edge. "Freedom of movement on Moore property. Freedom to operate your unique drones. I'd love to take a closer look at them sometime." Elijah tensed at the thought of his designs compromised. "But, as you know, we've suffered a major data breach. We're tightening all security. Your leeway has ended."

"No problem. Mr. Moore seems to be in no hurry to strike oil. I'm bummed. I was ready to help him find it." Elijah's only antidote for his surging adrenaline was to continue jousting.

"Your specialty," Julius said. "But you're a man of multiple interests. Rockets!" Elijah stopped his teardown.

"Along with drones, you like rockets," Julius neared Elijah, inspecting competition items on carts and tables. "You talk about them in your physics lectures. Lots of pictures in the decks you post. I'm sure many people would find your presentations interesting."

"You mean what I upload for the course?" Elijah felt Julius's full presence in person and online. "The portal is just for the students."

"And anyone with administrative privileges. But no one else, correct?" Julius said.

"Correct," Elijah said. The joust was over.

Julius nodded. He now stood inches from the motionless Elijah. "Good to see you're focused on edifying your charges right here." The voice that had boomed from the gym entrance was now constricted to a near-whisper.

"I'll steward my blessing," Elijah said.

With no handshake or goodbye, Julius left. Minutes later Elijah's breathing returned to normal. He'd essentially confessed to Jana his deduction that Baxter was building a launch pad, not an oil rig. He wondered if she'd alerted Julius. "Am I so smart?" Elijah knew the real answer.

Elijah's anxiety spiked anew. He pictured security rifling his room while Julius had occupied him in the gym. Moments later, he was in the basement apartment. All effects were undisturbed, his drones still roosted in the quiver. He reached in his desk drawer for the walkie-talkie.

"Mr. Moore, are you there?" Elijah said into the microphone. "It's me, Elijah."

"The drone master. I know who it is. I don't give out my gear to just anybody," Baxter II replied.

"Yeah, well about that. The security guy just came to see me. I'm busted for coming onto the ranch."

"He didn't say anything about me, did he?"

"Nope, but they're watching me. Not sure when I'll see you again."

"Everyone's uptight ... February 10 and what happens next."

"And just what is happening?"

"You're funny." Baxter II was still convinced Elijah knew more than he was letting on. "Everything's going according to plan, per the big message I received in 1985. My son has an army of people to see it through. I'll give you a shout if we need backup."

"Your family's project—" Elijah started.

"Ministry," Baxter II corrected.

"—your ministry goes back a long time." The old man's talk of action across decades and Baxter the third's now-unmistakable service tower entwined in his engineer's mind. He knew the Moores' interest in space was not a recent impulse.

"My dad started it when I was a little boy."

"Looks like I showed up at the perfect time." Elijah sighed.

"Isn't that the way!" Baxter II cackled.

The aircraft facilities at the Moore Ranch were active the next morning. Located at a far extent of the property, the runway had been stretched to more than 11,000 feet, sufficient for a jumbo jet. During construction, Baxter had publicly declared plans to receive oil drilling equipment via 747-8 freighters. Rumors flew that the enlarged strip would accommodate Air Force One so the president could hold secret meetings at the ranch. The extremist websites sparking Baxter's congressional reckoning had fanned speculation.

The queen of Baxter's personal airport was something barely half the length of a 747, a magnificent craft in its own right. The AtlasJet came from a conglomerate of business plane divisions sold off by manufacturers throughout the Americas. The plane could reach Mumbai from the ranch in a single hop, with a service ceiling of 50,000 feet and top speed approaching Mach 1. The cabin was wide, long, and regal, the rear portion comprising Baxter's mobile office and his bedroom.

Crowded into the office chamber were Baxter, chief engineer Wally Hastings, and Peter Farmer, a recent hire. Peter's title was purposefully vague—director of special projects. Further filling the space was Baxter's upgraded communications suite, a once-sleek console spoiled by added equipment.

"Everything the way you ordered," Wally told Baxter as he put a hand on the console. "Redundant interface with ranch IT systems, increased broadcast range, extra lithium-ion batteries housed in the cargo bay for max power. We've basically turned this bird into a flying command post."

"Mr. Moore, I assure you we'll handle the transmission from mission control," Peter said. "It won't matter if you're in the air."

"It matters to me." Baxter patted Wally on the shoulder and left the office chamber.

Wally followed Baxter into the main cabin, with Peter coming last. As Peter appeared in the doorway, Julius stepped into the aisle, blocking his path. The security chief glared at Peter for second-guessing the boss. He absorbed the message and sidled past Julius. The men vacated the aircraft, and Baxter dismissed Wally and Peter. With the sound of descending turbines, Baxter and Julius walked to the opening of the hangar housing the AtlasJet. A more prosaic business jet touched down and taxied to the apron.

Roy Parker and two junior attorneys exited. "I brought my top ninjas to work you over in the prep sessions." Roy shook Baxter's hand.

"That's what I'm paying you for," Baxter said.

For the remainder of the week, Roy and his team grilled Baxter in mock hearings, the sessions videoed and analyzed. Brad was part of the prep work as well, sitting at Baxter's side as he would be in Washington to provide him detailed website data per panel questions. By the time Sunday came, Baxter was ready for renewal and reflection at church services.

Pastor Humberto chose Romans 8:18 for the week's message: "'Yet what we suffer now is nothing compared to the glory he will reveal to us later.' We pray for the man who is our pillar of strength on earth, Baxter Moore, as he leaves for Washington, DC, today. May his trial—and I mean that in a biblical sense, not a legal one—be brief. May he emerge wiser and stronger from God's refining flame."

The worship team came onstage for a final song. Well-wishers shook Baxter's hand as he stood in his VIP seating area. Elijah pressed to the altar with those who worshiped on their feet. Jana came toward him.

"This can't be an enjoyable trip," Elijah said.

"I've been to the Hill many times. Baxter will do fine," Jana said.

"See you when you get back?"

Jana nodded and moved into the crowd. Elijah turned to see Brad behind him. Brad held up his palms, signaling no harm intended. The young men embraced, eager to dispel the tension between them. At midday, the AtlasJet took off for Washington, DC. Onboard were Baxter, Jana, Brad, Roy Parker and associates, and security team members. In just over two hours, the swift plane landed at Reagan National Airport. The entourage moved to waiting Suburbans and drove to the Watergate Hotel. Using a special entrance and elevator, Baxter went to the presidential suite, the other members of the party taking nearby rooms on the secure floor.

By sunset, the suite's long dining table was set for two. Hotel staff prepared the evening's meal in the private kitchen. Baxter stood on the balcony, warmed by the gas fire pit. Through the glass door, he saw a member of the security team usher a young woman into the suite.

Baxter came inside. "I can see why you wanted to go to college here. Glorious to be in the middle of American history."

"American history like the First Amendment? Yes, GW still believes in it, unlike my last school," Belinda Moore said, eliciting a headshake and a hug from her father. Baxter took an extra moment to observe the intricate design cut into Belinda's side-shave hairstyle, a look that would have been much less common at the Christian university she'd left two years prior. She shooed away the parental inspection.

Later in the evening, Baxter and Belinda sat at a corner of the dining table, allowing them to talk and take in the view while eating.

"Are you still mad at me and your mother?"

"Enraged." Belinda's dry delivery showed a lack of interest in her parents' divorce.

"How is she?" Baxter said.

"Happy, I guess. She's busy with her causes, one of which appears to be a boyfriend."

"Speaking of causes, have you chosen any good ones to support?"

"Is this a sneaky way to find out what I'm doing with my trust fund?"

"No, just shop talk, one philanthropist to another."

"I'm supporting a couple of groups. I keep my donations anonymous. I don't like calling attention to myself. And speaking of that, the bodyguards following me on campus are annoying."

"They're instructed to dress like students." Baxter earned an eye roll from his daughter.

"What's new at the ranch?" Belinda said. "You have more projects going on than anyone I know."

"Right now I'm focused on the public flogging that brings me to town."

"This too shall pass," Belinda said. "What about Brimstone 1?"

"Nothing much to report there."

"You always say that. I still see Grandpa climbing on the roof of the old house screaming about Brimstone 1, telling us to get ready."

"That was years ago, when his Alzheimer's was stage four. We're trying a new medication. I bought controlling interest in a biotech start-up. They have a promising approach—"

"I mention Brimstone 1 and you start talking about experimental drugs. The ol' pivot and bridge."

"Just practicing for tomorrow with the senator and her friends."

Dinner ended and Baxter walked Belinda through the suite foyer. "You can crash here," Baxter said. "Lord knows there's enough room."

"Group project meeting in the morning, super early. I should get back to the dorms." Belinda paused at the double doors. "Dad, why do you shut me out?"

"I'm not shutting you out. I'm protecting you," Baxter said. "The ministry your great-grandfather started will be revealed soon. I pray everything will make sense."

"Are we in danger?"

"Not you. But Grandpa and I were pulled into this. We didn't get a choice."

Belinda bristled. "You didn't give me choices either."

Baxter smiled sadly. "Sins of the father." He kissed Belinda on her forehead.

Against a red New Mexico sky, Tate sat in one of the rickety steel towers overlooking the mine ruins. His eyes traced railroad tracks threading a canyon toward the next valley, the location of the Moore Ranch. On his tablet, he read an email the law firm of Parker, Stone, and Kucera, "Mr. Moore will be unavailable until after the congressional hearing. We'll contact you if he is interested."

Breathing heavily from exertion and vertigo, Anik climbed the rungs to the lip of Tate's perch. He crawled to the middle of the platform.

"You're missing the view," Tate teased Anik who kept his eyes and center of gravity low. "Baxter Moore's lawyers just received a premium offer from a certain media company in Reykjavik."

"Or at least they thought they were talking to Iceland," Anik said.

"I'm bidding for our three favorite websites from Moore's portfolio. You know they've been great for recruiting. I'll double the offer after the hearing. He'll be dying to dump them by then. What happy news brings you up here?"

"The malware beaconed home," Anik said. "I relayed the go-ahead."

Cupping his mouth to imitate the sound of a loudspeaker, Tate said, “Ten, nine, eight—”

CHAPTER 8

The Central Hearing Facility at the Hart Senate Office Building was the premier venue for hearings on the Hill, providing ample space for congressional members, public audiences, and the media. Underscoring the media emphasis of the location, a green room was available for those called before lawmakers. Within this cloister, Baxter and his lawyers reviewed final details.

A door opened in the back wall and Baxter exited the green room, trailed by the others. The opposite wall was a marble slab, the imposing backdrop for the dais from which members of the House and Senate would make statements and pose questions. News cameras tracked Baxter as a compound eye as he made his way to the lonely table in front of the dais. The attorneys and Brad sat at a secondary table behind him to allow consultation during questioning. Baxter waved and smiled to Jana and several noted pastors sitting in the front row of the audience section before taking his place.

From the center seat on the dais, Sen. Fairchild rapped her gavel. "This hearing of the Subcommittee on Communication, Technology, Innovation and the Internet will come to order. A decade ago, America realized it was under assault on the internet, trapped in a torrent of fake news and divisive messaging designed to sow confusion and hatred." Baxter remained impassive, prepared to take verbal blows from the opening statement.

"Recently, we've learned Mr. Baxter Moore, one of the most powerful media figures in the country, secretly owns a number of websites publishing the types of content that harmed our country and made us doubt the institutions of government and a free press," Sen. Fairchild continued. "My colleagues and I have questions for you, Mr. Moore. Do you wish to make a statement first?"

"Senator, I submitted a brief written statement for the record," Baxter said. "I'm ready now for questions."

"As you wish. Mr. Moore, is *The Post* correct that you are the actual owner of the seventeen websites and social media platforms listed in its article?" The list appeared on a large screen visible to the room.

"Yes," Baxter said after briefly checking the list.

"Why did you conceal your ownership?"

"Under the laws of this country and the European Union, my decision to take ownership through holding companies was legal."

"Perhaps, but why the secrecy? The Moore brand is one of the strongest in the media industry."

"Exactly. My brand is very well-known. Our research showed that traditional media brands were unappealing to our target audiences. They wanted fresh perspective in their content and didn't feel they could get it from media companies that had been around for decades."

"Putting the people first. How thoughtful. And what made you pursue these target audiences?"

"I've diversified our audiences and business interests since I became an executive in my family's company after college. It's kept us ahead as media consumption has changed in the twenty-first century."

"You have diversified your family's holdings ... pharmaceuticals, oil exploration, aerospace ... that well-timed investment you urged your father to make in Google in 1999. It seems you're always looking for a new angle, Mr. Moore."

"My daughter would agree with you. She told me last night I have a lot of irons in the fire."

"I wonder if she'd also agree with me that your secret sites are factories for disinformation."

"I'm sure she'd disapprove of some and find others thought-provoking. I deliberately sought a broad spectrum of audiences and viewpoints. Users want to create and connect with content. They want dialog. This has been the direction of media for twenty years."

Elijah entered his classroom at Jeshimon Academy shortly before the morning bell. He set his drone quiver in a corner, not wanting it out of his sight after Julius's worrisome visit.

"I just talked to Mrs. Webster," Elijah said to his waiting students. Many of them were viewing the hearing on their mobile devices. "Anyone who wants to watch Mr. Moore's hearing may do so." He brought up the televised proceedings on the smart board. "If you want to study or read during this time, that's fine too. But let's stash the phones."

Elijah took a seat facing the screen. He wondered if the hearing would pry into Baxter's rocketry, a much bigger secret than the seventeen websites as far as he was concerned. Commentary whispered between the desks hewed to evangelical sentiment on social media: Baxter was under attack for being a Christian leader.

Sen. Fairchild continued questioning, "What is your revenue from the seventeen sites?"

Brad leaned forward to show Baxter the latest tally on his tablet. Baxter turned back to the table mic and said, "$114 million last fiscal year."

"So a small percentage of your overall income."

"It takes time to build ventures like these. Unique visitors have been steadily increasing until recently," Baxter said. He turned to glance at Brad's tablet again. "They jumped 400 percent after *The Post's* article and your announcement of this hearing. I'll have to raise my ad rates."

Sen. Fairchild gaveled the audience's laughter into silence. "What agenda are you pushing with these sites, Mr. Moore?"

"Every agenda and no agenda," Baxter insisted. "As *The Post* pointed out, these sites cover the left and the right."

"The extremes of both, you mean. Friends and enemies of the conservative Christian movement, of your company and family specifically. For example, you own the chat platform Moore Family Mysteries. Are you trying to control public criticism against you?"

"Do you see a lot of censorship on the chat?"

"No. In fact, I see little censorship across all the sites. Meanwhile, hate speech and fake news flourish."

"We have guidelines in place. It's hard to police all this content and uphold free speech."

"That's a tired argument. Other companies take reasonable care in what people do and see on their sites. You seem unwilling to responsibly manage these holdings. They are not a mainstay of your business. What's your endgame here, Mr. Moore?"

"I only have one endgame, the same one my family started eighty years ago: to spread the good news."

"Your sites have nothing to do with 'good news.'"

"Senator, in the past you've called me a Christian radical. Now I'm not being Christian enough?"

Elijah's class burst into laughter and applause echoing the display from sympathetic members of the hearing facility audience. Sen. Fairchild gaveled the outpouring before her. As the day dragged on, Baxter was grilled and praised according to the political stances of subsequent congressional questioners.

The verdict came early from pundits opining in real time: love him or hate him, Baxter Moore was a media master who could take the heat. Sen. Fairchild had overplayed her hand by failing to show Baxter was undermining American society with his seventeen sites. When the hearing ended, various participants sat for news interviews. Baxter wanted to return to New Mexico as soon as possible, but he knew he had to make the rounds to cement his PR victory. He spent additional time on the ground to fulfill media requests.

Night had fallen by the time the Moore party returned to Reagan National Airport. Baxter's private pilot, Capt. Melena, came out of the cockpit to speak to the passengers as they boarded the AtlasJet.

"Bad weather from Illinois to New Mexico," he said. "We should be able to climb above most of the chop. We could delay takeoff and wait for a break."

"Get us out of here," Baxter ordered.

Passengers took their seats in the main cabin. Baxter beckoned Jana into his office and shut the door. He sat at the communications console, and she took a nearby loveseat. Both fastened seatbelts built into the furniture. The AtlasJet taxied into position and took off steeply, seeking an altitude above the worst of the storm front, with the thinner air enabling top speed.

"Sen. Fairchild couldn't get the real answer out of you," Jana said. "I'd like to hear it."

"Ten years ago, AI analysis determined Brimstone 1 would be exposed before we were ready. No amount of security or secrecy could overcome the probability," Baxter said. "But by opening the floodgates for conspiracy theories about me, my business, and related topics, it would be harder to pick out the clues. We would increase the noise, to use a term from communication theory."

"So you were manipulating users. You did have an agenda. You lied to Congress," Jana said.

"The seventeen sites will be a footnote after we complete our mission and fulfill the ministry." Baxter worked at his console, not turning to view Jana's reaction.

When the plane leveled, Baxter opened a VPN tunnel to connect with mission control and ranch systems. Scaffolds and tarps no longer covered the long, low structure near Moore headquarters. The sign announcing a future museum was gone too. This day, the building assumed its true purpose as the Moore space center, housing mission control and other aspects of the Brimstone 1 project. Inside, Peter

Farmer led Brimstone 1 technicians. The highly automated systems required far fewer persons to manage than systems in the previous century's space race. Baxter began a video chat with Peter in his web link.

"Transmission window in nineteen minutes," Peter said.

"Message file loaded. I'll direct transmission from here."

Peter sent images to Baxter's screens—new pictures from the Israeli moon lander and a deep space photo with a large section of the moon occupying the corner as a reference.

"Lander photos show The Package leaving moon orbit as anticipated," Peter said. "The last shot is from the Lunar Gateway."

Under construction, the Lunar Gateway was a space station to support manned outposts on the moon's surface. Peter zoomed in on what appeared to be a speck in a photo from Lunar Gateway. The enhanced view showed The Package, tiny and indistinct, traveling away from the moon.

"It's coming." Baxter grew excited.

The AtlasJet lurched. "Sorry, Mr. Moore," Capt. Melena said over the intercom. "Updrafts from the storm system exceeding 50,000 feet. Pressure dropping fast over Missouri and Oklahoma. It's forming an eye."

"Bomb cyclone?" Jana asked as she stood behind Baxter.

"Yes, National Weather Service just confirmed," Capt. Melena said.

"We're flying into winter's equivalent of a hurricane," Jana told Baxter. The plane caught another updraft.

Elijah graded assignments in his apartment. He was logged into the student portal, digitally correcting papers. He noticed lags in viewing uploaded documents and recording his marks. Finally, the portal froze. He logged out and tried to reenter without success. Rain pinged in the corrugated well outside the basement window. The lights flickered, an insistent visual pattern alongside the rhythm of the raindrops. Elijah turned on a flashlight, wondering if the growing storm was disrupting the IT system. The screen on his school-issued laptop glowed red.

Frozen computers, red screens and flickering lights hit mission control as well. Peter issued verbal commands to his team, trying to clear systems. Now checked on wristwatches, the transmission window drew closer.

Baxter cursed as his airborne node suffered a similar crash. Standing beside him, Jana typed commands, trying to reset the computer.

"Can we transmit?" Baxter asked mission control.

"Negative," Peter said over the faltering video call. "Antenna control is locked out. Transmitters are inoperative."

Julius broke into the sputtering feed, his image appearing from the data center in the warren beneath Moore headquarters. "We're under cyberattack, denial of service. Some type of malware infecting all systems," he said.

"I'll override, transmit directly from the air," Baxter said.

"You'll never get a clean shot," Peter said.

"I have to try. Send a crew to the antennas and see if you can control them manually," Baxter said.

The walkie-talkie blared in Elijah's desk drawer. He lifted the radio to his ear. "Something weird is going on," Baxter II said.

"I think it's a cyberattack." Elijah checked the latest manifestations on his laptop screen.

"I think it's something more," Baxter II said. "See for yourself. You know my house, right?"

"Yes, but Mr. Moore, you need to contact your security team."

"I tried. Communication out. Please help me!" The typically feisty Baxter II was scared, which in turn alarmed Elijah.

Moments later, Elijah, in a rain poncho and heavy boots, drove through the growing storm, his drone quiver and gear piled in the passenger seat. His truck cleaved the flooded sections of road along the ranch's boundaries. Lightning illuminated desert vastness for split seconds amid the storm's blackness.

Clouds glowed and boiled beneath the AtlasJet. Updrafts lofted the plane despite its climb to its maximum service ceiling to avoid them.

"Crew can't get the antennas to budge," Peter's face in the video was a pixelated fog, the audio distorted and faint.

"I'll transmit from here," Baxter said. "How much time do we have left in the transmission window?"

"Twenty-nine minutes—" Peter's web communication cut off.

The malware had migrated to Baxter's airborne node as well. He struggled with his upgraded radio system. He lacked a large directional antenna on the jet but hoped he could signal The Package. Jana remained at Baxter's side, still attempting to coax the IT gear.

"I'm running out of ideas," Jana said. "We have maybe a minute before the system bricks."

Baxter pushed his transceiver to maximum power. The equipment quickly exceeded the command, digital meters pinning in the far red. Jana pulled Baxter away from the console before a blue flash erupted. Undetectable with human senses, the electric charge arced to the jet's metallic spine that channeled wiring within its carbon fiber fuselage. Afforded this pathway, the pulse shot to the cockpit. Cabin lights went out, and the plane pitched violently.

"Something just hit us," Capt. Melena said over the intercom.

"Lightning?" Baxter said.

"No, but we're losing cockpit systems," Capt. Melena said.

Baxter turned to Jana. "Could the malware do that?"

Jana shook her head. "The plane isn't tied into the ranch data center like your node."

Jana led Baxter into the main cabin toward the cockpit. The other passengers sat frozen in the pale emergency lights, tightening already-snug seatbelts, praying.

In the cockpit, Capt. Melena and his first officer labored to keep the plane level. The cockpit screens blinked on and off.

"Like I said, it wasn't lightning. But not even a lightning strike would do this," Capt. Melena said.

"EMP." Jana appraised the sputtering screens. "An electromagnetic pulse. All electrical systems are now frying themselves."

"Doesn't that require a nuclear explosion or a beam weapon?" Baxter said.

"Or a freak overload like we just had in your cabin," Jana said. "We made our own pulse."

"I've dealt with all kinds of nightmares, like that storm down there," Capt. Melena said. "But I've never flown through EMP."

"I have," Jana said.

The metal gate normally barring the driveway clanged in the wind. Elijah left his truck to lash the gate open, forearm raised to shield his face. He urged the Ram up the drive. The wash that curved around the house was a cataract, water lapping the wooden bridge. Elijah skidded to a stop close to the ranch house's front door, which Marta opened.

"Down here," Baxter II yelled from the basement. Elijah gave Marta a reassuring nod, aimed his flashlight into the tight stairwell, and descended.

Baxter II stood in a pool of light from an electric lantern. He tipped the lantern toward his 3D printer. "Did that come from hell?" he asked.

Elijah peered through the glass panel in the printer's front door to examine an object on the build plate. A small metal figurine leered back, a contorted, demonic creature with SATAN spelled in raised letters on its base.

Elijah removed the figurine and read aloud its complete inscription: "'Satan ... did not create this. Neither did God because neither exists. Sincerely, the true higher power.'" Elijah put the figurine in Baxter II's trembling hands. "Your cyber attacker is having a last laugh."

"Of course, they strike tonight. They knew about the transmission window." Baxter II tossed aside the figurine and tromped up the stairs with fresh resolve. "Thought I was crazy when I talked about needing backup? Come with me."

"Where are we going?" Elijah said.

"KNMR. Everything hooked to a computer is messed up."

"The old radio station? Now?"

"The message in 1985 was clear. If we don't send the signal at the right time, it won't come to Earth." Baxter grabbed gear bags from a hall closet.

"What won't come to Earth?"

"The Package. That's what we call it."

"What's that?"

"We'll never know if we miss the window."

Marta pleaded with Baxter II to stay inside. He patted her grasping hand and looked Elijah in the eye. "I'll go alone if I have to."

Baxter II stuffed his gear and Elijah's belongings behind the seats. One foot on the running board, Elijah heard a crash above the storm's din. He swung his flashlight toward the wooden bridge over the wash. An uprooted tree raked the structure. Water swirled until the timber was sucked into the flow, tearing away half the bridge's length. A narrow span of splintered boards remained above the roiling wash.

"We can't get across," Elijah yelled over the rain. He turned to find Baxter II vanished. A moment later, the old man returned, pushing his Harley from the garage.

"This'll get across!" Baxter II transferred gear from the truck to his saddlebags. Elijah slung his drone quiver on his back.

Elijah expected the old man to seize the handlebars. Baxter II pointed to his eyes. "Nyctalopia. I can't drive at night."

Elijah yelled in frustration and straddled the Harley. The only motorcycles he'd ridden were dirt bikes back in Williston. Baxter II took the seat behind him. Elijah started the Harley and moved out, hoping to go slowly over the broken bridge. The Harley wobbled. Elijah cranked the throttle and met the bridge hard. The wood groaned and cracked in the interminable seconds, supporting more than 1,000 pounds of men and machine. Bounding onto the wash's far bank, Baxter II sang "Born to be Wild" in his award-winning tenor as Elijah pointed toward the radio station.

Jana took the co-pilot's seat as Capt. Melena tried to keep the AtlasJet level. The first officer strapped into a jump seat in the rear of the cockpit as Jana donned a headset and checked controls.

"I can't keep the nose up," Capt. Melena said.

"That's all right. We want it pointing down, way down," Jana said. Capt. Melena and the first officer looked at her. "We need to shut off all systems before they burn up. That'll dissipate the pulse."

"The engines have backup generators. They'll stay lit on their own," Capt. Melena said.

"First officer, flip the circuit breakers on the generators. Complete shutdown," Jana said. "Captain, on my mark, set us at 50-degree pitch before we lose primary hydraulic control. We'll need maximum dive speed to windmill the engines and relight them. The AtlasJet has a ram air turbine generator, correct?" Capt. Melena and the first officer nodded. "We'll spin that core too and re-power systems."

Baxter braced himself in the cockpit doorway, listening to Jana's plan. "How long will it take to restart the plane?"

"We'll find out together. Let everyone know what we're doing," Jana said.

Cinching his seatbelt in the main cabin, Baxter notified the others of the deliberate descent. Moving to the bulkhead just outside the cockpit door, the first officer opened the circuit breaker panel. Jana turned off aircraft systems and signaled Capt. Melena to put the plane in a steep dive.

"She's all yours, commander," Capt. Melena said. The tops of the bomb cyclone's clouds filled the cockpit windshield.

"Flip the circuits," Jana called out. The first officer obeyed, and the AtlasJet went silent. New sounds prevailed—the airstream's whistle under acceleration and the thunder's roar—as the bomb cyclone swallowed the plane.

Elijah started the station's generator, and Baxter II activated the radio gear inside.

"I wanted to extend lead wires from the X-antenna to increase gain. Wish I'd finished that project before tonight." Baxter II hustled around the radio lab adjusting equipment. "Even forty years ago, I knew we were vulnerable with all the computerization." He looked toward heaven and spread his arms worshipfully. "No integrated circuits, no internet. Pop, you did it right!"

Baxter II pointed to a cabinet. "Grab the tape on the top shelf, upper left-hand corner, 'Message 2025' written in red marker."

Elijah handed the boxed reel-to-reel tape to Baxter II, who threaded the vintage tape deck.

Baxter II started the tape, a spliced loop of Bing Crosby reading James 1:17:

> Every good gift and every perfect gift is from above, and cometh down from the Father of lights, with whom is no variableness, neither shadow of turning.

As the verse repeated over speakers, Baxter II threw a final switch and donned headphones. "We're on the air! We'll get a reply when the message is received." Baxter II listened intently and frowned. "Nothing yet!"

The AtlasJet plummeted through the bomb cyclone clouds. The plane was fly-by-wire, using electronics to manipulate control services. With the shutdown, small, analog hydraulics still functioned, designed primarily to give pilots improved feel in their controls. Jana grappled with the vestigial system, trying to offset the violent buffeting from the storm. The plane began to corkscrew, eliciting new cries from the cabin. Jana tapped her fighter pilot and astronaut training to combat spatial disorientation, recognizing which direction was up despite the smothering clouds and blackened displays. She wrenched the plane from the worst wind current and stopped the roll.

"Dive time?" Jana shouted to the first officer.

"Forty-two seconds," the first officer responded, tracking the duration of descent on her wristwatch. From this, Jana could judge speed and altitude based on the last readings taken.

"No restart yet," Capt. Melena said as he listened for the engines. They were still lifeless.

"We need more speed. More pitch down, five degrees," Jana said.

Using the nominal hydraulics, Capt. Melena forced the plane into a steeper angle. The airstream noise raised in volume and tone. The cockpit screens blinked randomly.

"Ram air turbine is spinning," Jana said. "Close engine circuits."

The first officer struggled back to the bulkhead. She closed the circuits before sliding to the floor. The engines remained quiet.

Baxter II strained to hear a sound in his headphones. "Still no reply,"—he made more adjustments—"Lousy atmospherics aren't helping."

"Are the lead wires attached to the antenna?" Elijah said.

"Yeah, but they need to be extended and held tight. I didn't build the receiving structure."

Elijah grabbed his drone quiver and gear bag. He opened the radio lab door, allowing rain and wind inside the room. "Turn on your walkie-talkie." He headed into the storm.

Floodlights on the station building illuminated the X-antenna and the four lead lines. The bulk of each line was coiled at the antenna's base. Elijah located one free end at a time and reached into his quiver for a drone. Using the drones' roosting talons, he secured each wire to a craft. Soon, the drones flew in a slow formation to unspool the lead wires to their full length. The storm tossed the little craft, but Elijah kept the drones on course. Camera feeds confirmed talons gripping lead wires.

Jana and the other pilots heard a whine compete with the airstream noise. The AtlasJet's twin engines were relighting. Reactivated displays verified the turbines were back online. The altimeter was also among the displays now shining. Altitude was 1,200 feet and dropping fast.

"Full thrust and flaps," Jana commanded. Capt. Melena complied while Jana pulled up on the yolk. "We need to lose more speed. Lower landing gear."

As Capt. Melena held the yolk with both hands to assist Jana in arresting the dive, the first officer crawled to the controls and lowered the landing gear to increase the plane's drag. The plane's angle began to flatten. The wings shook with the conflict between the dive from 55,000 feet and a full-throttle ascent. The AtlasJet dropped through the bottom of the cloud cover. Lightning flashes revealed Oklahoma rangeland rushing to meet the plane.

"Now!" Elijah yelled into his walkie-talkie. His tablet showed the drones holding the lead lines taut 150 feet away from the antenna.

Baxter II cranked the amplifiers. The Crosby reading of James 1:17 looped. Baxter II pressed the headphones against his skull. Elijah heard him yell over the walkie-talkie and came running. The speakers switched from transmitter to receiver. An audio beacon played, a repetitive whoosh evoking a fetal heartbeat.

"Praise Jesus! That's it!" Baxter II shouted. Elijah joined him in a victory dance.

Jana could make out the honey mesquite shrubs before the nose finally tilted up. The plane re-entered the clouds and jounced in the turbulence, a mild disturbance compared to what the passengers had just endured.

Capt. Melena opened the intercom. "Thank you, God, for putting Commander McAlister on this plane. She is your hands and feet." The pilots and passengers cheered.

Baxter sat grimly, relieved to be alive but anguished over the failure to transmit. An ashen Brad approached him with a laptop.

"I can connect to the company system, at least the messaging app," Brad handed Baxter the computer, which he took back to his office. He tapped a joint message to Peter and Julius:

> **BAXTER**: Status?
>
> **JULIUS:** We're restoring systems. It may take days.
>
> **BAXTER**: Were you able to transmit?
>
> **PETER:** No. But there's something on a backup recorder.

Peter sent a link to the retrieved file. Baxter heard the Crosby snippet and the reply from The Package. He stifled an exclamation.

> **PETER**: That transmission didn't come from mission control.
>
> **BAXTER**: Find out who sent it. Verify The Package signal ASAP.

Baxter closed his eyes and wept.

Forty minutes later, Capt. Melena opened the intercom. "We're on final approach for the ranch. Flight control systems and landing gear are damaged. They've sprayed foam on the strip and we're expecting a belly landing. Please get in brace position."

Baxter still sat alone in his office. As he prepared to lean forward in his seat and lock hands behind his head, he looked out the window. The red beacon on the KNMR tower pierced the murk.

CHAPTER 9

In the middle of the night, Baxter entered his father's bedroom as Marta watched nervously from the hallway. He'd come straight from the airstrip where his AtlasJet lay rumpled on a bed of foam, passengers and crew brought home shaken but safe. Members of the security team examined equipment in the basement, muffled voices and occasional thumps rising from the stairwell.

Baxter turned on a nightstand lamp. His father was in bed, eyes closed, mouth agape, covers pulled up to his chin. Baxter whipped the bedclothes away, revealing a figure in muddy leathers and boots.

"Hey!" The elder Baxter groped for the covers. "I'm trying to sleep." He feigned a yawn.

The son grappled with his father for bedclothes. "The doctors told me brain plaques had dissolved. They wondered why you weren't showing progress."

"I don't want to be their lab rat," the old man said. "I'm staying put and out of sight."

"Wish granted." The younger man released the sheets. "News of your recovery can wait. We have other news to make first."

"The Package is coming! We heard the signal!" The old man sat upright, fully awake.

"No thanks to you."

"Who do you think sent the message?"

"Who do you think let malware into our system?" The

younger man stood to look his father in the eye. "Your 3D printer. Someone knew about it and sent infected firmware."

"I just wanted to—"

"Do your own thing? Stick it to the man? Still the hippie! You cost me a hundred-and-fifty million tonight between a wrecked jet and the IT restoration we'll need." Baxter watched his father's body sag and caught his breath. "But you redeemed yourself with that emergency broadcast. Welcome back, Dad." He put his arms around the old man and the two wept.

Elijah parked his truck near the gym. Upon hearing the landing jet, he'd rushed Baxter II to the ranch house and forded the receding wash to head home. He entered the building, dirty and exhausted. The internet-connected lights flickered, recovering with other systems from the hack. Elijah reached for the switch to illuminate the tiny hallway leading to his apartment. A hand extended from the shadows to flip the lights for him.

"Mr. Lindstrom, please come with me," Julius said.

"Are you arresting me? Can you even do that?" Elijah recovered from his start.

"Heeding my request would be voluntary, just as it would be voluntary for Mr. Moore to fire and sue you for gross misconduct," Julius said.

Elijah followed Julius out of the gym to the far edge of campus where a Suburban idled, two security team members in the front seats. Julius held out his hands to take possession of the items Elijah carried. Elijah relinquished his gear bag and slowly slid the drone quiver off his back. The two took the second-row seats, and the Suburban sped to the ranch.

Julius and the security detachment took Elijah to the level beneath Moore headquarters. Julius led Elijah into a small, sterile room, cameras at the corners of the ceiling its only adornment. They sat at a narrow conference table.

"Remarkable about Mr. Moore the elder. He was having sport with us. My team reported a 'scarecrow' darting about the ranch, but we never got proof."

"He approached me on my first day here. Asked me to keep his secret."

"Did he mention any other secrets?"

"You mean The Package? Didn't make a lot of sense. Maybe he's still 'having sport with us.'"

Julius weighed Elijah's response. He glanced at a message on his smart watch. "We're not through talking." Julius left the room.

Elijah removed his splattered poncho and undid the top buttons of his shirt. Julius hadn't confiscated his phone and he saw why—no cell reception under the building. The minutes stretched on.

Baxter entered with a tablet. "Elijah, I'm sorry for being heavy-handed. A lot has happened."

"Am I fired?" Elijah said.

"Far from it. I know you've been coming onto the ranch to test your oil exploration system. Yes, we looked at your drones. Brilliant." Baxter sat at the table and held up the tablet. "This is a deal memo. I want to license your intellectual property for twenty-five million dollars plus royalties on future sales and oil strikes made using the system."

"Why, when you're building a rocket, and we signaled an object coming from deep space?" Elijah replied.

Baxter gave Elijah a hard look. "Julius was right. You have figured it out. Did you come here knowing everything?"

"No. I came dreaming about what's on the tablet. Pretty funny now."

"Nothing's funny now. An anti-Christian militia called The Humanist League hacked us. The attack disabled my jet. We almost didn't make it."

"Is Jana —"

"She's fine like everyone else. She saved us."

"Does The Humanist League know the truth about what you're doing?"

"Much of it, I'm sure."

"Mr. Moore, you're running out of secrets. Is my silence worth so much at this point? That's what you're buying, not my inventions."

"Yes, I need your silence. And loyalty. In return, you have my gratitude. What you did with my father at the station is more important than you know."

"So if I sign on the dotted line, I can leave the room?" Elijah gazed at the tablet.

Baxter smiled. "Relax. Look over the memo. There will be some verbal additions, some special tasks. At the end of the school year, you'll have the money. I want you to complete your ministry at Jeshimon."

"Twenty-five million and a teacher's salary. Sweet," Elijah deadpanned.

Baxter stepped out. Elijah tipped his head back and closed his eyes, inserting prayers between waves of fear. More minutes passed before the door opened again.

"Back to play bad cop?" Elijah anticipated Julius's return—his eyes still shut.

"I'm off duty," Jana said.

Elijah jumped to his feet. He and Jana faced each other, unspeaking. Elijah was drenched and muddy. Jana's pulled-together look was undone—Ralph Lauren blazer held in one arm, long blond tresses escaping from a turquoise and silver clasp. They were both exhausted from their entwined ordeals.

"I heard you almost died tonight." A tear rolled down Elijah's cheek. "Is working for Baxter Moore worth it?"

"I made a deal." Jana shed her own tears. "I heard he offered you one too."

"Did he send you to talk me into it?"

Jana shook her head. "I'm just here to talk."

"Good. A few minutes ago, I imagined not talking to you ... ever again. Never seeing you again."

"When I brought the plane out of the dive, the first thing I thought about was having a long discussion with you."

"What would we discuss?"

"Electromagnetic pulses, cyberattacks, robots, drones—"

"Sounds romantic."

Jana laughed. "I knew you'd think so."

Elijah and Jana slowly closed the distance between them. They embraced.

"Has Baxter trapped us?" Elijah said. Jana arched her brows, leaving Elijah to draw the conclusion. "If we worked together, we could run away."

"I'm staying."

The embrace tightened. The first kiss was light, the second deeper.

"I'll stay too," Elijah said.

Jana allowed herself another kiss. "This is bad timing," she said. "By about twenty years." Undeterred, Elijah leaned in again. This time, Jana eased him back.

"You know who's watching," she said.

"God?" Elijah responded innocently. Jana restrained a laugh and pointed to the cameras in the room's high corners. "Let me give you some privacy to look over your paperwork."

Jana closed the interrogation room door behind her. Julius stood in the corridor.

"Did you enjoy the show?" Jana was icy.

"I already turned off the cameras and closed the observation room. I'm satisfied Mr. Lindstrom is no threat to the mission." Julius saluted Jana. She acknowledged and returned the gesture.

"Are you positive?" Tate said.

"I overheard Baxter. The transmission was made," Brad said. He had traveled to the mine for a pre-dawn debrief. "I just got a text. He's going to announce Brimstone 1."

"We'll stick to our original plan. Get back before you're missed," Tate said. "I'll be in touch."

"No, I'm done," Brad said.

"That's not up to you," Tate said. The bodyguards approached behind him.

"I just fell ten miles in a jet." Brad looked at the menacing men. "Your pit is nothing!"

The bodyguards moved on Brad, but Tate waved them off. He turned his back and walked into the mine's depths.

"Nothing!" Brad continued screaming—a lone silhouette in the maw of the shaft.

Reaching the League's workshop, Tate inspected the vehicles being hardened, and Anik joined him.

"Do you still think The Package is real?" Anik said.

"Baxter Moore's priority on the mystery transmission says it is. His bottomless budget does too," Tate said. "Are you going to argue again for a strike at liftoff?"

"No, I like your idea of hitting them at the happy homecoming," Anik said.

"Maximum emotional damage for the sheep cheering Baxter. Why is The Package bothering you?" Tate stopped at the flagship of his battle fleet, a line of flatbed rail cars. A steel-plated prow invoked the cow catcher of old locomotives.

"Maybe we should capture it. We could share it with the world, our way," Anik said.

"And the world learns eighty years of evangelism brought it to Earth, accomplishing what government and the scientific community have not," Tate said. "That would validate Jesus for billions of people, which has been the Moores's plan all along. We have to obliterate Brimstone 1 and anything it brings back from space."

"If The Package is real, that will be a loss."

"One more thing to blame on Christianity."

The leader of the rail car crew signaled Tate, and shaft occupants took cover. Lights dimmed, and an electric hum rose. Like fingers clenching into a fist, the hinged plates at the train's prow formed a battering ram. A second later, pistons punched the ram through a test barrier, spraying the shaft with wooden and metal fragments. Rising from his protective crouch, Tate led league members in applause.

At breakfast time Elijah returned to his apartment. He pumped his fist when he read Carla Webster's text about closing school for the day while IT services were restored. He was even happier reading the next text.

JANA: Did you get back all right?

ELIJAH: Just walked in with my drones, tablet, etc. I signed the deal memo.

JANA: Amazing what can happen under stress. Talking about Baxter making the offer, not your signature.

ELIJAH: Hope you didn't kiss me just because of stress. Don't know how I'd arrange an encore.

JANA: You know I didn't. But we need to talk about any encore.

ELIJAH: Oh no, here it comes.

JANA: Hold on. I'm asking you to be patient, discreet. I have a lot of eyes on me ... Baxter, his team, and soon the world.

ELIJAH: Do I embarrass you?

JANA: Elijah, I'm worried about embarrassing you!

ELIJAH: The "20 years" thing? If I'm going to be a millionaire, I can kiss who I want!

JANA: I hope money won't change you. THAT would spoil our encore.

Recharged with a few hours' sleep, Baxter readied a round of meetings in his conference room. Jana was seated for the first session, a video call.

"Please hold for the President of the United States," said the White House operator.

From his Oval Office desk, the president said, "Baxter, glad you're in one piece. Heard the trip home was a lot rougher than your time before the joint committee."

"No sweat when you have the greatest pilot since Chuck Yeager." Baxter smiled at Jana.

"Nice work as always, commander," the president said.

"Thank you, Mr. President," Jana replied.

"My confidence in Brimstone 1 remains high," the president said. "You have the best astronaut, the best technology. But I'm worried about your security."

"It's the best too. Granted our adversaries have landed a few blows, but we've knocked them back," Baxter said.

"We both have a lot riding on this program. Godspeed on your first flight," the president said.

"With many more to come, sir," Baxter said. The president ended the call.

"Why is Brimstone 1 so important to the president?" Jana said.

"A list of foreign and domestic customers for future missions. They want no publicity, no questions asked regarding their payloads. The president wants plausible deniability while advancing his space policy. I'm the perfect contractor," Baxter said. "In turn, we got federal approvals practically overnight that would've taken years, including using the ranch as a launch site."

"Does the president know about The Package?"

"I'll read him in at the appropriate time."

Jana remained stoic at Baxter's admission of playing the executive branch as he'd played the legislative branch during the hearing.

"We have our first big announcement to worry about," he said before activating the intercom. "Donna, please send in the team."

Baxter's inner circle filed into the conference room featuring Julius, mission control director Peter Farmer, Moore Media anchor Tanya Cummings, and attorney Roy Parker. Elijah was on the invite list too. He took a secondary seat along the back wall. Peter looked askance at his entrance, contrasting with the warm smile Jana gave him. Brad was the last to arrive. He sat next to Elijah.

"You look like hell, bro," Elijah whispered to him.

"Long night for all of us," Brad whispered back.

Baxter stood before the assemblage. "We're under assault. Today, we leave the shadows and take the initiative. We're announcing Brimstone 1. We're accelerating the timetable for launch. Update, Julius?"

"IT restoration in thirty hours. Doing forensics on the malware artifacts. Implementing new cyber and physical security protocols," Julius said.

"Good. Tanya?"

"News division is ready for your reveal segment. Staff is on standby. And I have great questions to ask you,"

"I bet," Baxter said. "While we're talking about media ... Brad?"

"Dark site on Brimstone 1 ready to go live. Content is current. I'll collect photos and clips from the news division for immediate posting," said Brad.

"Keep the hourly sentiment reports coming. Increase surveys," Baxter said. "Peter?"

"Mission control systems will be fully restored along with overall IT. Conducting final inspections on hardware. We'll be ready for transport to Rig Alpha in five days," Peter said.

"Are you sure? I know I'm rushing your people," Baxter said.

"Yes, I'm sure." Peter looked back toward Elijah. "I see Mr. Lindstrom is now part of the launch team. If we have any trouble putting the rocket in firing position, I'll ask if he can raise it with his drones."

Peter's comment prompted muted laughs. Baxter walked toward him, his salesman smile at full intensity. "Among many things, Brimstone 1 represents a learning opportunity. I've made Elijah mission ambassador to Christian students around the world. Careful, Peter. He might discover some engineering prodigies and you'll be out of a job." Robust laughter filled the room. Jana gave Elijah a sly glance.

After the meeting adjourned, attendees conversed in small groups. Roy Parker came alongside Baxter. "We're getting a lot of buyer interest in the seventeen websites," he said.

"Make the best deals you can, but sell them fast," Baxter said.

"Congratulations on your new assignment," Jana said to Elijah. "Your classroom is going global."

"Students will want to hear from Brimstone 1's pilot," Elijah said. "I'll be in touch."

"Looking forward to a long discussion," Jana said.

"Exciting times, right?" Brad said to Elijah.

"Yeah. Must feel good having everything out in the open." Elijah clasped Brad on the shoulder.

Tate sat in bed at his shuttered motel. Marissa slept beside him. Tate smiled at the email from Baxter's law firm. His offer for the three sites was accepted. In his cover as an Icelandic media company, Tate had asked to see the backend of the largest site to prove its value through user totals and extent of collected data. The request was granted.

Tate reveled in his behind-the-scenes inspection. The data trove revealed users' web behavior and psychological traits, a huge assist for Humanist League recruiting. The purchase brought one more victory—ownership of the same site where Tate worked as a content moderator, the digital abyss that had swallowed him a decade earlier. Now he held control.

Eager to exploit his new online holdings, Tate opened the file for a "news story" he'd prepared:

CHRISTIANS SEIZING CONTROL OF OUTER SPACE!

America's most powerful Christians are not running away from science. They are seizing control of outer space, "the final frontier," to promote their mythology. Christians have developed secret technology to interfere with scientific satellites and publish doctored orbital photos to "prove" the world is flat and was created in six literal days.

Tate nudged Marissa awake. "Check it out. Here's the story I had you write."

The content blended her provocative text with polished visuals, including the logo of a fictitious news agency. She smiled and nestled against Tate.

"Now a quick user sample." Tate used his AI software to identify users most likely to engage and share the story. "And it's tomorrow's must-read." With final commands, Tate scheduled the story for the users' feeds.

"Let's see who's curious," Marissa said.

"Like you were curious?" Tate said. The young woman recalled the content that had first caught her attention. A series of subsequent clicks drew her deeper, eventually leading to a suitcase hastily packed the night before her eighteenth birthday. Hiding and working in the mine was exhausting but exciting. She had come to crave invitations to the Motel Apocalypse since her first visit.

"I'm still curious," Marissa reassured her leader-turned-lover before closing her eyes.

Baxter sat in the library under his headquarters. He read an update from Roy Parker that three sites had been sold, with the rest expected to go within a week. Logging into the digital archive, he opened two video files side by side. a black-and-white taping of his grandfather and a color clip of his father.

"To my successors, I've transmitted God's Word across his creation. And I've received an answer, a small, still voice from beyond our world," Baxter I said. With his skinny tie and thick glasses, he resembled the midcentury scientists and engineers he'd abandoned to enter Christian broadcasting.

Baxter paused his grandfather's message from 1960 and played his father's message from 1985. The clip showed a robust Baxter II in early forties, his musician's beard and locks shorn but a thick mustache retained.

"After nearly forty years of broadcasting including twenty-five years of direct messages, we now know something is coming, the physical proof to share with a broken world," Baxter II said. "It'll take another forty years to arrive, enough time to figure out how to receive it properly."

Baxter toggled between the two recordings, mouthing the memorized words of his ancestors. "This is a prophecy for the twentieth century and I'm sure, the twenty-first," Baxter's grandfather proclaimed. "This is your true inheritance."

"Be the one who receives the glory from the heavens," Baxter's father said.

CHAPTER 10

"I'm Tanya Cummings, Moore Media News, with a major announcement from Baxter Moore, the CEO of this network." The director switched to a two-shot of Baxter seated next to Tanya.

"I'm launching a rocket from my New Mexico property, a private venture called Brimstone 1," Baxter said. "We're using boosters and components manufactured by a variety of companies. Brimstone 1 is a combination of proven systems modified and integrated for our program specifications."

While Baxter continued speaking, the feed switched to an artist's rendition of Brimstone 1, a two-stage rocket topped with an orbital vehicle. "The orbiter is a spaceplane with a cargo bay, similar to the space shuttle but smaller." The animation zoomed in the wedge-shaped craft. "This will be a manned flight, piloted by Commander Jana McAlister."

The feed returned to the two-shot of Baxter and Tanya. "Why are you going into space?" Tanya asked.

"Commercial space flight is a signature industry of the twenty-first century. I've diversified my family's holdings for years. Not that I don't enjoy being your boss, Tanya, but media is only a portion of what we do."

"What will be Brimstone 1's first mission?"

"We're deploying a series of cubesats, tiny satellites, to start a new communications network called Urim. It will be devoted to Christian content and interaction."

"Communications? That gets back to your family's core business."

"True," Baxter replied. "Our initial efforts will establish a space-based network to deliver Christian content around the world. Most people connect to the internet through mobile devices. This is the case especially in developing nations, where we need to vigorously preach the gospel. The challenges and successes we've seen with our new programming in Indonesia bear this out."

"Would you call Brimstone 1 a Christian rocket?"

"Everything I have belongs to the Lord. Yes, it's a space venture dedicated to Christian ideals. At the same time, customers will be able to hire us for secular payloads on future launches."

"Let's take an actual look at Brimstone 1," Tanya said. The director switched to a live shot from the rocket site. "What are we seeing?"

"This is Rig Alpha, located on my ranch," Baxter said in voiceover. "It's the launch area for Brimstone 1." A slow pan showed the complex while Baxter described its features. "That's the service tower. Over there are the fuel storage tanks. And here's the Horizontal Integration Building. This is where we stored sections sent from the factory in Texas and assembled the vehicle."

Cameras turned to a Quonset hut bigger than a football field. The videographers walked to the open end. Sand dunes filled the space, the material used in fracking. A mound split open, revealing what appeared to be a sand mass as a fiberglass camouflage. Steel doors opened to a tunnel. The videographers entered the passage.

The building interior yawned like a cathedral nave. Inside, the components of Brimstone 1 lay horizontal. The rocket's stainless-steel fuselage gleamed under work lights, protective tarps covering certain portions. Tailfins arched toward the building's ceiling and walls. Visually, Baxter's rocket was a throwback to the lustrous V-2 derivatives gracing his grandfather's pulp magazines at the radio station.

"These are the booster stages," Baxter said. "Brimstone 1 will be 260 feet tall on the launchpad, producing nearly two-million pounds of thrust. The first stage is reusable. It will land in Texas after stage separation."

A videographer paralleled the prone boosters, tracking their silvered skin in detail. Another jumped on one of the bicycles technicians used to traverse the cavernous space. He dismounted and captured the bell-nozzle cluster protruding from the bottom of the first stage. The third approached the orbiter parked alongside the boosters. The length of a school bus, the manned vehicle invoked a mashup of a conical capsule and delta-wing jet. The main wings were steeply raked and stubby. A smaller pair protruded from the orbiter's dorsal side. The four wings' tips extended past the rear of the fuselage, forming tailfins in the manner of the first stage booster.

"This is the orbiter. We'll deploy the cubesats from the cargo bay and touch down on the ranch runway," Baxter said.

"We? Who's flying with Commander McAlister?" Tanya said.

"I am. I paid for it. I get to ride shotgun."

The director returned to the studio shot. "Social media commentary on Brimstone 1 is already heavy," Tanya said. "Here's a post from Sen. Iona Fairchild." The content appeared on the screen:

> @USSenatorFairchild
>
> Just when we thought Baxter Moore had nothing left to hide, now comes his rocket Brimstone 1. When does your secrecy stop, Mr. Moore?

The screen streamed other posts from ordinary citizens either angry or cynical about Brimstone 1:

This is dangerous technology to put in the hands of Christian kooks.

Another private rocket ... big deal. As if Baxter Moore wasn't rich enough already.

The president has given Moore a nuke to drop on San Francisco. The fire to go with brimstone. Sodom/Gomorrah 2.0.

"You said you were searching for shale oil to explain the heavy construction, cargo jets landing at your strip, freight trains unloading along the spur on your property," Tanya said. "Everything at the launch site was built to look like oil production structures. Why the elaborate ruse?" The screen showed stills of the Rig Alpha complex with titles over:

SERVICE TOWER/OIL RIG

**ROCKET FUEL TANKS/
FRACKING WASTE RECOVERY TANKS**

**VERTICAL INTEGRATION BUILDING/
EQUIPMENT AND SUPPLY WAREHOUSE**

"Anti-Christian groups have become aggressive, one militia in particular. I'm their declared target. They want to destroy me and my interests. I have a lot to protect," Baxter said.

"You suffered a major cyberattack two days ago, correct?"

Baxter nodded. "It disabled my jet, and we almost didn't make it. Perhaps Sen. Fairchild can explain her perfect timing in bringing me to Capitol Hill. Because of her, we were in the air and helpless during the attack. Any secrets in that scenario? You tell me."

"Is your timing to announce Brimstone 1 based on that near-disaster?"

"Yes. As I told my launch team, we're coming out of the shadows. Brimstone 1 is not simply a multi-billion-dollar rocket. It's an instrument of God."

"To be balanced, here are some social media posts praising Brimstone 1," said Tanya. A stream of pro-Moore comments appeared on the screen:

BRIMSTONE 1 IS THE NEW CHARIOT OF FIRE.

WAVE TO JESUS FOR US, BROTHER BAXTER!

GOD WATCH OVER BRIMSTONE 1! PRAYERS FOR COMM. MCALISTER AND MR. MOORE!

ROCKETS AND SATELLITES TO SERVE THE LORD. ABOUT TIME. #BRIMSTONE1

"This ministry needs the support of God's people," Baxter said. "We'll need plenty of prayers from liftoff to landing."

Sen. Fairchild switched off the broadcast in her office. "Why do I have to watch TV to learn Baxter Moore is going into outer space?"

"My source only gave me information on the websites," said Krista Simon, her chief of staff.

"I look clueless investigating the sites when he's hiding something much bigger," Sen. Fairchild said. "He can't be launching rockets without cooperation from the federal government. I want to know who's backing him! Who's protecting him!"

Krista checked her phone during her boss's tirade. "Senator, we may need to slow down on Baxter Moore. New poll is in. Thirty-nine percent overall say you were part of a conspiracy to crash his jet. Sixty-eight percent say so in the rural counties of our state."

"Part of a conspiracy? I would need information. I would need a plan. Does that sound like me right now?"

Krista left the senator fuming in her office. She slipped into an empty office in the Hart Building. "The Senator is losing it," she said into her phone. "She thinks she was fed the website info to look weak and out-of-touch on Baxter Moore."

"She is weak and out-of-touch," Tate replied from the mine. "Moore owned her in the hearing."

"You've got to get me something on Brimstone 1!" Krista said.

"Moore and his security have gone into beast mode," Tate said. "No more hacks, leaks, or half-measures. And no more calls from you."

Tate hung up on Krista. He walked to the pedestal rock in the hub room. The Humanist League members sat around the stone in their silent circle, viewing the Brimstone 1 segment on their mobile devices.

"Have we seen enough?" Tate asked. The circle mass-clicked *Y* for yes. "The next time we have a watch party for Moore Media, they'll be airing Baxter's funeral!"

"Well, Dad, you went public." Belinda's video call captured the bustle at the Square 80 Plaza on The George Washington University campus.

"It was time," Baxter said. "I'm getting a new jet delivered from the factory. I'd love to fly you back for a visit."

"Dad, I can't right now."

"Besides me, there's someone else who'd like to see you." Baxter turned the view on his phone toward the living room of the old ranch house.

"Hello, sweetie," Baxter II smiled and waved from an easy chair.

"Grandpa?" Belinda started crying.

"I'm Elijah Lindstrom, It's my pleasure to be your educational guide to Brimstone 1, Baxter Moore's space project." Elijah spoke into a webcam, starting a live stream. "I'm coming to you from Jeshimon Academy in New Mexico. Today, you'll join the lecture and group exercise in our physics class. Say hello, everyone." Elijah's students smiled and waved at the webcam.

Elijah recapped rocketry examples he'd used to illustrate physics principles in previous lectures. He glanced at his web feed. The image behind him of the classroom's back wall and smart board disappeared, replaced by an electronically produced background. A hastily drawn cartoon depicted a crooked skyrocket emitting puny puffs of smoke. Titles above blinked:

Space is for scientists, not religious fanatics!

Elijah calmly approached the computer and deleted the protest background. "Note to whoever just hacked us ... it's not free speech when you interfere with ours." His live students cheered.

Baxter watched a delayed feed of Elijah's Brimstone 1 education channel. He clicked pause and smiled. "Elijah's a natural. Handled that well. What's happening in the rest of the world?"

"Sentiment levels holding," Brad said. "Our base strongly supports Brimstone 1, especially if it's used for Christian purposes. "Opposition metrics are decreasing somewhat. You won sympathy points for nearly dying in a plane crash."

"Any change in threat level?"

"No boost in number of online threats or users liking them," Julius said. "Latest negative keyword is 'unrisen.' We're tracking it closely."

"Getting back to Elijah, he's going live in a Moore Media interview," Brad said. Baxter enlarged the news channel's window on the media wall.

A minicam team interviewed Elijah and Carla outside Jeshimon Academy as parents picked up their children. A pickup truck sped into the front parking lot. A person stood in the bed and hurled projectiles. Elijah shielded Carla as the objects splattered the group red. The truck escaped as school security came running.

"Water balloons with paint in them." Julius surveyed the scene from the media wall view. He called school security as Baxter cursed.

Brad covered his mouth with his hands, first thinking the crimson spray was from gunshot wounds. His stomach churned. He dreaded putting his old friend in harm's way.

Shaking paint off his hands and arms, Elijah gingerly withdrew his phone to check an incoming message:

> **BAXTER:** Welcome to the front lines. Send me your dry-cleaning bill.

In the early evening, Elijah towel-dried his hair. His mother was on a video call, having seen the protest drive-by on TV.

"You were great," Teri said.

"Even when I was getting paint-bombed?" Elijah hung up the towel and looked into the phone propped on top of his dresser.

"Especially then," Teri said. "You were very gallant protecting your headmaster."

"Good career move." Elijah laughed.

"At least you know why Moore didn't give you a petroleum job," Duane sat up in bed, mustering strength to speak.

"I'm still convinced he has deposits on the ranch, strange as that sounds," Elijah said. "Someday, we may go looking for them."

"Now, he wants you to be an internet personality as well as a teacher?" Duane said. "I hope you got a raise."

"He's making it worth my while." Elijah smiled at his oblique reference to the pending windfall from Baxter. He marveled at how financial security made it easy to deflect his father's gruff remarks.

"And you get to work with Commander McAlister," Teri said. "I remember she was your hero during middle school."

"That was half my life ago, Mom." Staying low-key about earnings and Jana was difficult, but both the signed NDA and promise of discretion bound Elijah.

Duane began coughing. "It's time for your father's nebulizer," Teri said. "Congratulations."

Julius broke in with a video call as Elijah finished talking to his parents. "May I see you at the headquarters building?"

"Am I in trouble again?"

"Should you be?"

Julius received Elijah in his office. "Sorry about your mishap at school. We're adding a gate on the private road leading to the driveway." He handed Elijah a small manila envelope. "Your upgraded security card is inside."

"No more sneaking onto the ranch," Elijah said.

Julius smiled. "Please let us know whenever you want to visit Rig Alpha. You'll still need an escort."

"Understood. Do I have permission to visit the old ranch house?" Julius nodded.

By early evening, Elijah was at the Dunromin Travel Center picking up a large to-go order. The hostess brought the bags of food to the front.

"You're Commander McAlister's friend," the hostess said. "How's she doing?"

"Great." Elijah took the bags.

"Now we know why a famous astronaut is in town. Brimstone 1! It's been all the talk around here," the hostess said. "Please tell her I'm praying for her."

Elijah set the food into the passenger seat and footwell. He messaged Jana:

> **ELIJAH**: The hostess at Dunromin said she's praying for you. Speaking of which, how about dinner ... discreet, I promise.

Baxter II brought firewood from a shed near his detached garage. Elijah stoked the pile already burning in the long-dormant fire pit. He handed a Dunromin meal to Marta who was sitting in a lawn chair. The sunset was ending, and the night air was still. Jana walked around the house to join the group, boots and jeans as always but wearing a Ralph Lauren shearling coat in place of one of the brand's blazers, topped with a cashmere muffler.

"Nothing like the smell of a good piñon fire," Jana said.

"There's a real New Mexican," Baxter II said. "Welcome to my home."

"Happy to be here," Jana said. "It's been forever since I've enjoyed a bonfire."

"Me too." Baxter II placed split logs in the blaze. "Don't have to worry about sending smoke signals to my son or anyone else now."

Elijah handed a meal container to Jana. She smiled, recognizing the same menu item she'd ordered during their interrupted dinner at the Dunromin. The fire climbed the logs that had been curing in the woodshed for years. The foursome silently prayed and dug into their meals.

"I have a lot of questions about Brimstone 1's history," Jana said. "I've been going over the archives."

"I digitized my father's notes and files decades ago," Baxter II said. "My son continued the process. We did a good job preserving everything. We knew one day there'd be a reckoning."

"But there's nothing like living testimony," Elijah said. "I'd like to learn more too. I should interview you on the education channel when the time's right."

"I'm just the bridge in the Brimstone story," Baxter II said. "Dad was the scientist. Baxter the third is the entrepreneur. I'm a storyteller, nothing more. If I could, I'd still be on the road with my band, the J-Men. We were big in the days when they called it 'Jesus Music.'"

"Don't let him fool you," Marta said. "This one is smart too. When I was a little girl, we'd watch the Moore family's

TV shows. My parents read the Christian magazines they published in Spanish. He did all that."

"The good ol' '80s. Cable was booming. Print was in its prime. Just more ways to tell stories," Baxter II said. "More ways to acquire treasure for this ministry. I knew we had another forty years to go."

"Did you think at first you'd have to partner with NASA?" Jana said.

"Yes, not that we wanted to. The Moores may get cozy with government, but we don't trust 'em. Goes back to what my father saw on the Manhattan Project," Baxter II said. "Then my son graduated college, and he had a lot of new ideas. He said private spaceflight would become feasible. We could launch our own vehicle, use our own crew."

The evening drifted on. The foursome finished the dinner and desserts from Dunromin. Sipping coffee from the ranch house kitchen, they turned out their lawn chairs to witness the starscape over the ranch. Baxter II strummed his Martin D-28, the acoustic guitar his mother had given him for his eighteenth birthday. He sang a mix of Christian and pop songs, a catalog more than a half-century old.

Baxter II began "Everything I Own" by Bread. The romantic ballad had been a hit twenty-seven years before Elijah was born, but its effect jumped generations. He and Jana were sitting slightly behind Baxter II and Marta, shadows deepening as the bonfire ebbed. Elijah reached to Jana and she took his hand, one more discreet touch.

The lyrics ended and Baxter II continued the chords. "Commander, you bring yourself and my boy back safely." The old man's voice choked. Elijah and Jana looked at each other, hands locked, eyes glistening.

CHAPTER 11

"Ten minutes!" Anik shouted.

The Humanist League scurried down the main shaft, dragging equipment and vehicles into the deeper reaches. The mine exterior and the first hundred yards of the primary subterranean corridor betrayed no human presence. Anik oversaw final efforts as League members gathered in the hub room, some in night-vision goggles pointing weapons toward the terminus of the main shaft, the path to the surface.

"Fuel cell power down in five, four, three—" Anik said into a handset. At the appointed moment, the mine went dark and silent as its power source ceased operation.

In the valley where the derelict mine stood, the seldom-used rail lines vibrated. A slow freight pulled a dozen flatbed cars, a delivery from the California company that had made the service tower. A narrow metal structure resembling a blade stretched more than 200 feet long on gimbaled mounts across several cars. A helicopter from the Moore Ranch swung into view and flew low escort over the engine for what would be the last miles of the journey.

While Anik had led the League to the hub room hundreds of feet below ground, Tate had climbed to the perch in the mine site's tallest tower. Concealed on the platform, he relished the clandestine view of the ranch-bound train, the security helicopter oblivious to his aerie in its close pass. Tate watched the train disappear into the narrow canyon exiting his valley. He tapped a message to Anik:

TATE: In the canyon. Minimize movement until train has left the area.

Once through the canyon, the train turned onto the spur line that bisected the ranch. It passed the airstrip and halted at the point closest to Rig Alpha. A crew lifted the blade off the train with twin cranes and consolidated it with the rest of the train's cargo to create a mammoth road vehicle, the transporter erector, the machine to place Brimstone 1 in firing position. A drivers' cab commanded two autonomous engine cars supporting the blade, each rolling on honeycombed, airless tires. Baxter had insisted on a costly vehicle design that could be promptly deployed like a mobile missile launcher while having the strength to handle a rocket almost as tall as the US Capitol dome. As the transporter erector rumbled to life, the train backed down the spur to retrace the canyon.

While Julius looked on, crew members emplaced a steel barrier across the tracks at the ranch's border. "Spur is sealed," Julius said into his handset.

"Copy," the security team member said on the other end. "Transporter erector heading into position."

At the Horizontal Integration Building, truck-mounted cranes cleared the sand mound decoy and tunnel module. Huge plastic curtains retracted on motorized runners, and Brimstone 1 was visible to the outside world.

The transporter erector eased into the building's opening. Peter Farmer's technicians had met the five-day deadline, and the assembled Brimstone 1 awaited the first part of its voyage. The orbiter was mated to the boosters, and the entire spacecraft rested in a scaffold cradle. Progress came in inches as the transporter erector's blade inserted precisely into the rocket cradle. During the painstaking process, crew members removed the solid back wall of the Horizontal Integration Building, affording a view of the long, wide road to the service tower.

Dusk came, and launch team principals gathered at Rig Alpha. "Ready for carriage," the crew chief announced over loudspeakers.

Hydraulic cylinders hissed and metal groaned when the mass of Brimstone 1 shifted to the transporter erector. The giant tires bulged as they took the weight. Crew members inspected critical points along the vehicle, all relaying affirmative reports.

"Go for tower," the voice said over the speakers.

The transporter erector backed Brimstone 1 out of the building, tires squealing on the concrete floor. With Moore Media broadcasting every step, TV audiences around the world cheered as the bottom edges of the tailfins and the bell-nozzle cluster cleared the structure. Floodlights blazed along the transport road and up the sides of the service tower. Brimstone 1's slow procession would take the night.

"For I can do everything through Christ, who gives me strength," Baxter said to the television audience. "Eighty years ago, my grandfather bought a small radio station. Tonight, we jump to the stars."

"Do you think your grandfather would've imagined this moment?" Tanya said.

"Yes."

Moore Media camera teams moved about the Horizontal Integration Building as the vault gradually emptied of Brimstone 1. They captured more comments from Baxter, Jana, and Peter. Elijah shadowed the teams, careful not to interfere with their news-gathering and live broadcasting. Collecting shots and insights for his education channel, he walked toward Peter to get a quote, but the flight director conspicuously turned away.

Undaunted, Elijah went to the crew chief whose loudspeaker announcements had signaled the rocket's take-up and haul. Elijah asked him different sets of questions intended for audiences based on age—lever principles to tilt the rocket for grade schoolers; for grad students, materials science facts about the transporter erector's lift rating. He would edit and tag the clips later for upload to the online channel.

Jana came close to Elijah for a quiet moment along the building's curved wall. "How does it feel being on the inside?"

"Better than tiptoeing around on the outside," Elijah said.

"Just remember, the real education starts for all of us when we land," Jana said.

"Yes, Brimstone 1 is a recovery mission," Elijah added.

Jana put a finger to his lips, reinforcing the layer of secrets behind the rocket's debut.

The transporter erector continued its inexorable trek to the tower. Two drivers functioned as pilot and co-pilot in the cab, the orbiter's belly twenty feet above their heads. The drivers used a series of cameras mounted on the vehicle and pacing drones to obtain visuals, while crew members walked alongside for extra vantage. The audience dropped off as only the most ardent viewers stayed tuned to what was the globe's slowest motoring attraction.

After several hours, the transporter erector reached its designated spot at the foot of the service tower. More time passed as crew members anchored the vehicle to lift Brimstone 1.

"Go for tilt," the crew chief said.

Powerful pistons tipped the blade, and the rocket nosed skyward. The end of the blade slid into a multi-ton steel and concrete receiver positioned over the flame trench at the tower's bottom. The receiver, blade, and cradle stayed in tandem with Brimstone 1, forming the gantry that would bring fuel and electrical power to the rocket on the pad. Hold-down arms on the pad waited until the rocket pivoted into their grasp.

"Rocket at five degrees," the crew chief said. "Close clamps." With Brimstone 1 now nearly vertical, the huge clamps closed on the tailfins.

"Transporter, pull back." At the crew chief's signal, the transporter erector's motorized components retreated from the service tower.

By dawn, Brimstone 1 assumed the iconic spacecraft stance at Rig Alpha, umbilicals linked to the gantry. Vapor seeped from valves on the boosters' sides as technicians began pressure tests on fuel tanks. The protective tarps had fallen away during the lift, revealing the rocket's livery: "Brimstone 1" written in a blue vertical font with bands of repeating cross symbols above and below the fifty-foot logo. The New Mexico sunrise played on the silver ship, burnishing an image shared by millions in minutes on social media.

Members of the launch team walked the service road, talking excitedly about their accomplishment. Jana stood alone, appraising the craft she would pilot.

"Smile for me," Elijah said, camera ready. Jana turned, radiant, Brimstone 1 gleaming behind her.

The rollout concluded, Elijah returned to his apartment. Fueled by adrenaline and a pot of coffee, he quickly showered and dressed for the day. The walkie-talkie sounded in his desk.

"Well done," Baxter II said over the speaker. "I liked your education updates more than the official line from Moore Media."

"Appreciate it," Elijah said. "Speaking of education, I still have to teach my classes. Got to make this fast."

"My son demands I limit my e-commerce. He also took away my 3D printer. Can I send you to the local swap meet for some motorcycle parts?"

"Sure. Email me your list." Elijah set the walkie-talkie on the desk and cocked his ear while he finished buttoning his shirt.

"Thanks, buddy. As soon as I'm cleared to be seen in public, we'll hit the swap meet together. I could tell you some stories from when the place was still a drive-in. Yours truly had an Impala convertible, 348 engine with three deuce carbs."

"I bet you made quite an impression," Elijah said.

Once Elijah was in the classroom, his students were fascinated to learn more about Brimstone 1 and his experience at the rocket's rollout. He answered their questions patiently while advancing his lesson plans. Brad arrived during his physics class to take social media shots of Elijah teaching.

"Bro, you're trending," Brad said after the bell, lifting his tablet to show web user stats on Elijah's education channel for Brimstone 1.

Shiloh overheard Brad's announcement. "You can't see how many times I've logged in, can you?" she asked. She laughed and waved goodbye to Elijah.

"I'm one tiny part of the Brimstone machine." Elijah began packing his gear. "I'm going to the swap meet this Saturday. Want to come with?"

Brad shook his head. "I've got all the turquoise jewelry and macrame I need."

"Just thought it would be a good chance to hang. We haven't done that in a while."

"Maybe something else, soon." Brad slid his tablet into a backpack. "Meanwhile, I have to stoke the Brimstone machine, as you put it."

At his apartment, Elijah yearned for sleep but didn't want to crash too early and wake in the middle of the night. He reviewed Baxter II's emailed parts list. Primary was an exhaust pipe to replace one that had been damaged in the wild ride to the station. Baxter II concluded his message: "Last time I let you ride my Harley!"

Elijah looked up vendors advertised as swap meet regulars. He shared the specifications of what Baxter II wanted. All promised to be on the lookout for Baxter's pieces and urged Elijah to meet them at the show. He then started thinking about shopping for himself, not at a swap meet, and after his 25 million dollars arrived. A search flurry brought up equipment for a private engineering lab and fully optioned pickup trucks. Elijah stopped himself. He whispered a prayer and created a spreadsheet in an encrypted folder. He began making categories:

- Big River Church, Williston: $2,500,000

- Taxes: TBD
- Mom and Dad:

At first, Elijah was pleased with his turn in fiscal planning, but unease soon engulfed him. So much money steeped in secrecy must have pitfalls. Would Baxter and his lawyers find a way to renege once Brimstone 1 was over? Was he breaking the law by taking what was obviously hush money? Would people mock his education channel if they knew what he was getting from Baxter? An incoming message broke his cycle of worry and warranted a response:

> **Brad**: IMS for being a jerk about the swap meet. Let's do something sophisticated like play video games. Just like old times.
>
> **Elijah**: Yeah, I'll kick your butt, just like old times.

Elijah knew his exhausted brain was flailing. He shut down all devices, turned off the lights, and burrowed into bed.

The hectic school week ended, and Elijah looked forward to the swap meet's simple diversion. Baxter II had sent two thousand dollars with a message to Elijah to get something for himself as well. Elijah had converted the electronic transfer into a stack of twenties, knowing the bazaar would prefer cash. A vendor messaged him early Saturday morning:

> **Hogback Hogs**: Dude, jackpot, stall 42!

Elijah pulled up to the ancient drive-in. The movie screen still stood, its back expanse a faded mural proclaiming the Enchantress Drive-In Theatre. A Native American maiden in a buckskin miniskirt posed on a boulder overlooking the desert. The objectifying, politically incorrect image had stirred controversy for years, but the property owners refused to demolish it, arguing instead for recontextualization. The owners allowed dense graffiti and informal monuments along the bottom of the mural protesting its depiction of women and indigenous peoples, converting the site into an exhibit for tolerance.

Elijah parked his truck and joined the throngs perusing wares. Vendor stands occupied the spaces where cars used to park to watch the show, many of the stanchions for cast-metal car speakers still in place, rusted and canted. The aromas of hot dogs and street tacos competed as Elijah walked past the food stalls. At the stand for Hogback Hogs, the proprietor greeted him across a folding table.

"Just got my hands on this last night." He hefted a cylindrical object covered with a blanket. The blanket pulled away to reveal a pristine exhaust pipe, heavily chromed with a special filigree design.

Elijah took a photo and sent it to Baxter II. The old man replied immediately: "Don't come home without it."

Elijah paid Hogback Hogs top dollar and tucked the find under his arm. He spotted a stand with Christian memorabilia—jewelry, artwork, milk crates full of vinyl records. Elijah pondered buying Jana a small item but worried about crossing an emotional line. He thumbed the albums by Christian artists from the '60s through the '80s. He spotted one by the J-Men, Baxter II's old group. As the front man, a young Baxter II was center of the cover—dark, flowing hair and beard, a cherry-red Stratocaster strapped across him.

"They were great," the stall operator said. "Saw them open for Larry Norman when I was a kid."

Elijah set aside the album. He anticipated the hoot of having Baxter II sign the front. Elijah looked at women's jewelry. A ring would be excessive, but maybe a charm bracelet. He could add baubles post-Brimstone, a means to mull the future.

"If I had a Christian girlfriend, I'd go with that," a voice said from behind.

Elijah turned. The figure behind him was medium height, with hood pulled up and sunglasses. The "gray man" was studiously unremarkable. His most distinctive attribute was a face covering, which some continued to wear after the pandemic.

"Thanks for the advice," Elijah said. The bracelet slipped from his fingers back to its velvet pad.

"You're welcome, Elijah."

Startled by the stranger calling him by name, Elijah left the stall, the J-Men album forgotten. The gray man followed.

"Don't freak. I don't have any water balloons." The gray man laughed. You're a quasi-celebrity on that education channel." Elijah slowed his pace, preparing to respond. "Of course, I knew who you were before then. Now you can freak."

Elijah and the gray man stopped in an open area away from the stalls. Pedestrian traffic was light in this corner of the drive-in grounds. The stranger pointed at Elijah's chest. A red dot shined there.

"Don't run, yell, or reach for your phone," the gray man said. "And don't swing that fancy tailpipe at me."

"You could've paid a kid five bucks to tag me with a laser pointer," Elijah said.

"Or I could've paid a grownup far more to aim an M24 rifle with a laser sight at you."

Elijah surveyed the lot, his eyes locking on the movie screen. The beam emanated from that direction.

"Triangulation and analysis: top of the old screen, hollow inside with ladders and platforms. Perfect sniper's perch. You think quickly," the gray man said.

"You too. This ambush opportunity only came up recently," Elijah said.

"It isn't an ambush. It's a conversation. I still want you to join us."

"The Humanist League. I remember your micro-targeted ad."

"We're built from people like you, intelligent people who were forced into Christianity."

"Can't be smart and believe in Jesus? I've heard that one before." Elijah's eyes darted. No one was nearby, no one could help.

"You're a smug bunch at the ranch. Baxter Moore will not jumpstart Christianity with Brimstone 1."

"He's launching a commercial rocket, not a revival."

"Spare me the cover story. And spare yourself a lost cause." The gray man's fervor increased, resembling ranting in the hub room. "You were impressive the night of the hack. But you still haven't realized your potential."

"Is this the part where you tell me to come to the Dark Side?" Elijah said.

"No, because you're already on the Dark Side. I was in a family that beats Bibles ... and kids."

"I grew up in a Christian home. I didn't suffer child abuse."

"Depends on what you call abuse. I know—and you know—what it's like to run every thought, every brilliant idea past a fake god and the people who speak for him." The gray man poked Elijah in the chest near the laser dot. Elijah was ready to drive a fist through his face covering but stayed motionless as warned.

"Don't you dare be smarter than your dad or your pastor. When you get older, don't second-guess your angel investor, your billionaire boss, Jesus Christ." The gray man gave Elijah some space. "After 2,000 years, we'll destroy the mythology crushing true human genius. Today, we have the weapons to fight back."

"The internet," Elijah said. "History's greatest mind-control device."

"I don't control minds. I nurture them. I free them. Normally it takes months and an appropriate distance to grow my best candidates. I'm making an exception for you."

"Like you said, spare yourself a lost cause."

"When the fire comes, remember the bargain you turned down at the swap meet," the gray man said. "Watch the dot."

Elijah stared at the laser light still trained on his chest as the gray man merged with the crowd. He remained rigid until the dot vanished. Elijah sank to his knees.

"Who knew you'd be at the swap meet?" Julius said. Elijah was in his office, reporting the encounter.

"Mr. Moore's father, obviously. Probably Marta. Brad, a couple of parts vendors I contacted. Emails and messages," Elijah said. "Do you think they've hacked us again?"

"Always possible, but we've added protections," Julius said.

"Maybe the guy just followed me."

"Stationing a sniper indicates they had advance knowledge of your movements."

"If there was a sniper." Elijah wasn't sure which was worse, being in crosshairs or being tricked.

"You were right to take him at his word," Julius said. "Very bold of The Humanist League. First physical contact we've documented."

"Why would they try to recruit me?"

"Ego. They call themselves a militia, but they're really a cult. If that was their leader, he's displaying an invincibility complex. He thinks he can come into the open, exert power over anyone. And if you don't defect, it's still a psychological victory. You tell the organization what happened, we get rattled."

"What should I do?" Elijah asked.

"Just what you've been doing. Don't let them disrupt you. When you're going to town, let me know. I'll have some of my people go with you."

"Brad said I was trending. Time for an entourage?"

"Time to be on guard. Wartime."

CHAPTER 12

"The Package is secure. Run sensors." Jana tapped a screen to close the orbiter's cargo bay. The panorama of Earth unrolled in the cockpit windows.

Baxter activated the sensor array in the hold. The display indicated the sensors were scanning The Package for microbes and radiation. An alarm sounded.

"Pathogens detected," a programmed warning said. A second alarm, louder and shriller, went off. "Pathogen breach in cockpit," the warning repeated.

Jana slumped in her seat. "Point Nemo," she whispered.

Baxter called up the pre-programmed flight plan. A digital map displayed an arc to a destination in the South Pacific—Point Nemo, coordinates in open water, equidistant from New Zealand, Chile, and Antarctica. Baxter tapped the final command. The cockpit view jarred, and the orbiter pointed its nose toward Earth.

"It'll be over soon." Jana's head was to one side.

The reentry angle was calculated to incinerate the orbiter, crew, and cargo many miles above the ocean. As the spot farthest from land masses and their inhabitants, Point Nemo was the preferred "grave" for unmanned spacecraft ending their missions—and an ideal terminus for a condemned manned vehicle. The blue void of the Pacific beckoned as tiny bands of fire encircled the orbiter's windshield panes.

Jana sat up and turned off the alarms. With more taps, the view of Earth went blank. A recorded voice announced, "simulation terminated." Jana and Baxter uncoupled their harnesses and stretched. Bright lights turned on beyond the windshield.

"I hope everyone's worked up an appetite," said Baxter, checking his smart watch. "Barbecue is ready."

"Claw control is lagging," Jana said. "Let's test it again after lunch."

Jana flexed a haptic glove she wore. On a screen, the claw on the cargo bay's robotic arm mimicked the movement of her fingers. From his workstation, a mission control technician appeared on another screen. Wearing a glove identical to Jana's, he manipulated the claw in the same manner.

"I'll run some diagnostics using the backup glove," the technician said. "Then we'll try your controller again."

Jana and Baxter exited the hatch and climbed down metal stairs beside the simulator. The orbiter facsimile sat in a chamber spanning basement to roof inside the space center. Peter Farmer met the astronauts at the bottom of the stairway.

"Same trusty vehicle you flew to ISS, Commander?"

"With some nice upgrades. Excellent response on the new maneuvering thrusters," Jana said.

"How did I do?" Baxter said.

"You saved Earth from alien contamination," Jana said. "Not bad for a day's work."

After the barbecue lunch and more simulator time, Baxter and Jana went to the library underneath headquarters. Baxter selected an audio file:

> Second response, first acknowledgment of bilateral communication: April 1973
>
> "Still listening to Holy Bible. Please continue," the voice from space said in the recording. The timbre was hollow, and the pitch wavered, but there was emotion, connectedness. "Thank you for keeping secrecy."

Jana paused the recording. "The sender knew their secret was safe, otherwise earth media would've been filled with the news." Baxter nodded, and she restarted the file.

> "Love Creator. Need Creator. Need faith. We die without it. 'Now faith is the substance of things hoped for, the evidence of things not seen.' Hebrews, Chapter 11."

"I hear sadness, desperation," Jana said.

"The sender wasn't the only one feeling that," Baxter said. He selected another file:

Baxter I reply to second response: April 1973

> "I'll transmit the Bible continuously. I'll maintain your need for secrecy, but please explain. Tell me more about yourself," Baxter I in the recording. "I rejoice that you love the Lord. Rely on him for strength as I do. You talk about dying. This may be the last time you hear from me. I have terminal cancer. My son will have to continue in my place. I pray he will take up this ministry."

"Then your grandfather told your father," Jana said.

"'The special talk' you heard about on the demo tape," Baxter said. "The next communication from the sender was the longest of them all, the announcement of The Package coming to Earth. It ended with this." Baxter summoned the key message and skipped to the end of the file:

Third Response, Announcement of The Package: April 1985

> "Yes, I understand death. I hope to see you in heaven. You've shown me the way there," the sender said in the recording.

"Dad turned communication over to me in 1997," Baxter said. "We got another message, and I responded. I identified myself as the grandson and said we'd be ready to receive what was coming. There was one more transmission." Baxter opened the final file:

Fifth Response: January 2010

"Faith, hope, and—" the sender said. The transmission faded before the final utterance.

"I responded again. We should've received a new message by 2022 ... 2023 at the latest. There's been nothing more," Baxter said.

"Are you sure the sender is still alive?" Jana said.

"We don't know. We don't know who or what the sender is. We asked for more information as you've heard, but the responses were usually brief."

"Did you worry it was a hoax?" Jana said.

"We did. Were the communists taunting us for our beliefs? That thought was extra motivation to keep quiet during the Cold War. Now, The Package has shown up when promised. No hoax. No turning back."

Launch preparation for Brimstone 1 accelerated. Baxter wanted liftoff close to Easter with little notice to keep protestors and The Humanist League off balance. Super-cold nitrogen filled the rocket's tanks in cryogenic tests to replicate fueling and launch stresses. Testing progressed over the weeks. A "wet dress rehearsal" placed an actual fuel load into the rocket. One major hurdle remained.

"Within the next twenty-four hours, we'll conduct a static test of Brimstone 1's main engines," Baxter said in a Moore Media special announcement. "If you live within thirty miles of the ranch, you'll hear a loud roar and feel the vibration. This is normal ... and exciting."

At noon the next day, the boosters lit, the hold-down arms clamping the fins to keep the rocket on the ground. The flame trench at the base of the service tower filled with orange, boiling exhaust, and a white cloud billowed hundreds of feet.

Baxter and Jana watched the test from an observation bunker. Occupants cheered when the burn stopped, the rocket intact, the test a success. Baxter's mobile phone rang.

"My name is Baxter Moore the second, and I want to lodge a complaint. That rocket test knocked my Strat off its stand." The old man was unable to suppress a laugh.

"Sir, if you'd had that guitar strapped on your body, the way I always remember you, it wouldn't have fallen," Baxter said.

Days later, a line of vans from Jeshimon Academy drove onto the ranch. Security waved them toward the launch complex. The vans parked on the broad service road between the Horizon Integration Building and the service tower. Students and staff disembarked to enjoy the closest public view of Brimstone 1 yet allowed. A security helicopter slowly circled the launch complex as the school field trip approached the rocket, phones held out to take photos and video.

Elijah held back as his students surged forward. Were he ten years younger and had a similar opportunity, he would have led the pack. Now he was content to observe the enthusiasm his lessons had instilled in his students.

"Still disappointed you ended up in the classroom instead of the oil fields?" Carla's presence startled him.

"Not really. I guess this must be how parents feel when they watch their kids develop and grow."

"Speaking of parents and kids, I just spoke to Mrs. Garcia," Carla said. "The pregnancy is going smoothly. She wants to take sabbatical next school year. Would you be available for more teaching?"

"That's very kind," Elijah said. "Can I think about it?"

"Sure," Carla said. "I know Brimstone 1 has changed a lot of things."

Two cyclists ascended a mountain bike path in the late afternoon. The man spurred his Giant Fathom, determined to reach the crest first. The woman on a matching bicycle pedaled harder. A dog yelped excitedly, cutting off the man and allowing the woman to win the sprint.

"No fair! I don't have a K9 partner," Julius said.

"Blue doesn't want you to get too far," Wanda said. "I see you little enough as it is."

The pair got off their bikes, laughing. Wanda poured Blue a drink in a collapsible water bowl before having her own swig. Julius took her in his arms, and Wanda playfully flicked water at him.

"Now you're both ganging up on me," Julius said. "I deserve it."

"I'll take you whenever I can get you. It's good to see you unwind."

"It never stops, love." Julius retrieved the water bottle mounted on his bike. "Every time I think we've fended off The Humanist League, they take a new approach. I've fought the Taliban, al Qaeda, ISIS. I know the signs. They're probing, waiting."

"They don't know what they're in for." Standing behind him, Wanda put her arms around Julius's waist, careful not to disturb his Jericho in open carry.

"You know the old line. Terrorists only have to get it right one time."

Inside the main mine shaft, a League team rolled a railroad truck, the chassis holding wheelsets normally seen underneath a railcar. They positioned the truck on the rails leading to the surface. Standing alone, the truck resembled a large metal dolly. The crew took cover along with other League observers in the shaft.

"Power up," Tate said to Anik, who repeated the command into a handset.

The lights in the shaft dimmed as they had for the test of the battering ram. The fuel cell array generated a maximum load. The rails in the shift rang with the current. The truck trembled and clattered before accelerating like a catapult-launched jet. The wheeled assembly shrieked along the rails, bursting from the mine opening and arcing skyward, unable to hold the turn into the small switchyard outside the shaft. The truck flew forty yards before crashing into a dilapidated shed below the steel towers.

League members cheered. Marissa looked at him with reverence. Tate clasped Anik on the shoulder.

"Let's get our own launch ready," Tate said.

"Welcome to today's livestream on the Brimstone 1 education channel." Elijah spoke into a camera on a tripod. "Today, we have Brimstone 1's pilot, Commander Jana McAlister, to take questions from our viewers."

Directing the live stream from a desk holding a laptop and tablet, Brad switched to a two-shot from another tripod-mounted camera. Elijah looked at a large monitor out of the cameras' view to read teleprompter notes.

"Let's go to Mrs. Yvette Bishop's third grade class at Hillcrest School in Ohio," he said.

The livestream went to dual screens featuring the third graders at Hillcrest and Elijah and Jana at Jeshimon. The students cheered when they saw themselves on the feed. A girl stepped up to read a prepared question from a small digital tablet.

"Commander McAlister, I want to be an astronaut like you when I grow up," the girl said. "When did you know you wanted to be an astronaut? What should kids do to become astronauts?"

"Great questions," Jana said. "When I started grade school, Sally Ride became America's first woman astronaut. I grew up in Clovis, New Mexico, near Cannon Air Force Base, and I watched different kinds of aircraft zoom over the town. By the time I was your age, I wanted to fly, all the way into space." The girl smiled at Jana's account of her childhood.

"Math and science are very important if you want to be an astronaut." Jana turned to Elijah. "Several years ago, I helped a Christian group called 'Out of This World Science Club' teach kids. Elijah was in the program. How old were you?"

"Thirteen," said Elijah.

"And you know how smart he is, if you've been watching this channel. To get into astronaut training, you can become a pilot like me. I learned to fly jets in the US Navy. Or you can become a mission specialist like Dr. Ride. Scientists, engineers and physicians can be astronauts too."

"I'm good at math," the girl said. The teacher nodded and classmates giggled.

"Then you're off to an excellent start. Good luck," Jana said.

"Next we have students from Great Plains Christian University in Nebraska, my undergrad alma mater," Elijah said. The split screen switched to a group in a study room. They waved when their image came up. "What's your question for Commander McAlister?"

"Actually, my question is for you, Elijah," a young woman said. "My name is Molly, and I'm an education major. How do you like teaching?"

"I really like it, but I sort of fell into it," Elijah said. "My youth group went on a mission trip to Minneapolis when I was in high school, doing street ministry. My pastor asked me to teach the neighborhood kids we were serving. He said, 'You can't sing or play guitar, so I can't put you on the worship team.'" The students laughed. "I've taught science, robotics and math since then, on other mission trips, at camps, and now here at Jeshimon Academy. You should talk to my mom. She's been an elementary school teacher for almost thirty years."

"I bet she's proud of you," Molly said.

"That's what she says, every time we talk," Elijah said. A group "aw" rose from the college students.

"One more question. What do you think of this?" Molly switched the view of her study group to a screenshot of her computer. "It's a fan page!"

Entitled "Elijah Lindstrom, Awesome Christian Teacher," the social media page featured photos and video of Elijah curated from the education channel. A text block presented James 3:1:

> Dear brothers and sisters, not many of you should become teachers in the church, for we who teach will be judged more strictly.

Elijah put his hand to his mouth. Jana clapped and said, "Looks like you've stumped the awesome Christian teacher. I think the page rocks." Molly and the study group whooped.

After dinner, Elijah graded assignments in his apartment. He welcomed the sessions as they help him forget how Brimstone 1 had changed everything, as Carla had said. A message chimed:

> **Brad**: Thirsty?

Brad included a map share of his current location, an unfamiliar spot far outside Todos Santos showing no meeting places like restaurants or coffeehouses. Elijah worried about his safety after the swap meet incident, but he worried more about Brad. Elijah messaged back:

> **Elijah**: Three more papers to grade, then I'll swing by. Where are you anyway?

> **Brad**: Just drive where I showed you. Can't miss it.

Later that evening, Elijah pulled up to the abandoned motel. The gate across the driveway was open, allowing him to park alongside Brad's car. Elijah checked the directions and confirmed he was in the right place. Light emanated from room 7. The door ajar, he knocked, then peered inside. Brad was sitting at a tiny, circular table near the drawn curtain. A 24-pack of beer was ripped open at his feet, several empties teetering on the table.

"I thought so." Elijah surveyed Brad's state. "The last time you asked if I was 'thirsty' was grad night."

"We talked about doing something for old times' sake," Brad said.

Elijah waved off a proffered can as he sat. "What is this place?"

"A very exclusive establishment."

"A very closed establishment. Are you even supposed to be here?"

"I have connections." Brad cracked the beer he was going to give Elijah.

"Bro, you're good for now." Elijah gently took the beer from Brad's grasp.

"I didn't ask you here to spoil the fun," Brad said.

"Why did you ask me here?"

"I want to apologize for bringing you to New Mexico under false pretenses. There was never any oil exploration, and I knew it."

"Really? We're way past that. Everything turned out fine."

Tate watched the meeting in the dingy motel room from a monitor in his mine office. "Oh, Brad, I was about to send you a more entertaining guest."

"Do you want us to take them?" Tate's lead bodyguard said.

"Baxter would lose it if two of his tribe went missing. We don't need search parties combing the desert," Tate said. "Brad hasn't said anything damaging yet."

Brad stood abruptly, scattering empty beer cans. "You don't understand! I brought you here. I brought you to Brimstone 1!"

"And I thank you," Elijah said.

"You'll live to regret it ... God willing," Brad said.

Elijah put his hands on Brad's shoulders. "You're not making sense, which is understandable. Let me take you home."

"I have something to tell you—" Brad resisted Elijah's efforts to lead him away.

Tate's lead bodyguard stiffened. Tate held up a hand, signaling calm.

"If it's important, wait 'til you're sober," Elijah said. Brad kept crying and mumbling that he was sorry as Elijah herded him out of the room.

"That's our Elijah, the servant leader, just as I profiled him." Tate watched room 7 go dark on the monitor. "If they head for the mine, intercept them. Otherwise, let our so-called asset sleep it off."

Saturday morning, Elijah prepared his breakfast smoothie in the kitchenette. His phone chimed:

Brad: Thanks for saving me from myself last night.

Elijah: How worried should I be about you?

Brad: I survived grad night. I'll get through this.

Elijah: Do you need a ride to pick up your car?

Brad: No. I'll handle that. Thx. Want to hang later today?

Elijah: Sorry, bro. Busy. But let's get together soon... BYOB: Bring Your Own Bible.

In the late morning, Elijah and Jana's trucks came down a dirt road from opposite directions. They parked at the bottom of a trail that wrapped a large mesa. Both dressed for hiking, the pair embraced at the trail head.

"Follow me," Jana said.

The path rose and narrowed, eroding to barely shoulder-width in several places. Elijah turned his body toward the mesa wall to traverse the most treacherous stretches. When the path widened again, Elijah jogged to come alongside Jana.

"This is not a hike I would've picked," Elijah said.

"And the best part is coming," Jana said.

The path ended ten yards below the mesa rim. A tight cleft awaited. Jana used its many crags as handholds and footrests to make the final climb. Elijah clambered behind her. The pair reached the summit. Elijah braced his elbows on his knees, sweat dripping off his face. Jana dabbed his forehead and took his hand. She led him through a stand of boulders to the mesa's broad expanse.

Elijah and Jana reached the far rim moments later. The Moore Ranch spread below them, all landmarks visible—Brimstone 1 a glinting knife blade in the distance, the headquarters office complex, the space center, the long runway where the orbiter would return to Earth.

"I picked this spot for you," Jana said. "We'll have plenty of coverage at the runway. You can shoot the landing from up here. Capture the final glide path through the valley."

"And I thought you brought me up here just to be discreet." Elijah turned from the vista and looked at Jana. They kissed deeply.

"The encore," Jana said. "Feel better now?"

"Yeah," Elijah said. "You?"

Jana pondered. "Yes and no." She slipped from the embrace and walked to the edge of the mesa.

"I thought you're OK with this," Elijah said.

"I am, and that's the issue," Jana said. "It's the craziest thing I've done outside of a cockpit."

"And crazy is bad?"

"For me. Being selfish is worse. To continue the flying references, I don't want to take you off course."

"Away from my predictable life?" Elijah said. "Stay in my hometown, marry the boss's niece. I blew up that plan before I came to New Mexico, before I met you."

"You could restart the plan. Look up that sweet education major in Nebraska. She's crushing on you, if you couldn't tell. Take her home to meet your mom."

"That's not what I want."

"You want your pinup girl!"

Elijah walked to the edge where Jana stood. "So I'm acting out a fantasy?"

"Maybe. Maybe I am too. Gorgeous, younger man. Super intelligent. Christian. You check a lot of boxes."

"I'm flattered. But I wasn't your pinup," Elijah said. "Who was?"

Jana grimaced. "Jason Priestly, 90210."

Elijah smiled. "What would you have done if Jason Priestly had walked into your life years later?"

"When I was your age? I would've said, 'Get lost. I have jets to fly and a master's degree to finish.'"

"You had a plan and stuck to it. So much for trying to put you in my shoes," Elijah said. "What's your plan now?"

"As soon as I'm wheels down with Brimstone 1, I'm heading back to Clovis to finish building my therapy ranch," Jana said.

"And you're not leaving any room for—?" Elijah motioned in the space between himself and Jana, unsure of the words to use. Us? Love?

"I'm going to help people overcome their pain and regret," Jana said. "I don't want to be your regret."

"Then be selfish," Elijah said. Tears forming, Jana grabbed Elijah's shirt, drew him close, and kissed him.

CHAPTER 13

Jana and Baxter were in the simulator, clad in sleek, light-gray spacesuits. The mission patch rode their shoulders—the rocket lifting off, exhaust and a light flare creating a cross image, the circular banner proclaiming "Brimstone 1. The First Christian Rocket." The countdown clock reached zero, and the simulator shuddered, replicating liftoff sensations. Computer-generated images of exhaust engulfing the pad enhanced the training environment.

"Abort! Abort!" a voice said over the speakers.

Jana pulled a lever in the middle of the control panel, one of the few analog instruments in the cockpit. A simulated force exceeding standard liftoff slammed the astronauts. Images showed a belt of emergency rockets around the orbiter's middle igniting, separating it from the rest of the spacecraft. On-screen, the launchpad image morphed into a mammoth fireball as the boosters "failed catastrophically." The orbiter arced from the destruction, and Jana began a slow, vertical descent. Stubby legs popped from the winglets' trailing edges, and the craft alighted on a virtual landing pad two miles beyond the flaming launch complex.

The simulator lowered from its nose-up position. Jana and Baxter uncoupled the communication and pressure lines from their suits and left the cockpit. Peter Farmer and several technicians were waiting for them on the floor of the simulator chamber.

"Thought I'd throw you a curve," Peter said.

"I hope you enjoyed it," Baxter said with a nervous laugh. "I didn't."

"Have to rehearse the good and the bad," Jana said.

"Pray for the first one, please." Baxter joined hands with Jana. Peter and the technicians closed the prayer circle.

"Heavenly Father, may we grow closer to you in body, mind, and spirit during our upcoming flight," Jana said. "May Brimstone 1 be remembered as a mission to glorify you. All this we pray in your name." The circle said amen.

That afternoon, Belinda entered the old ranch house. Baxter, his father, and Elijah were having iced tea and snacks.

"There's my girl." Baxter II reached out for a hug.

"I still can't believe it." Belinda took in her restored grandfather.

"Remember, not a peep about Grandpa until Brimstone 1 is wrapped up." Baxter gave his daughter a peck on the cheek. "We don't need any more eyes on us." He motioned Elijah over.

"Ah, the education channel guy." Belinda shook hands with Elijah.

"You've been watching?"

"Yes. I think your content is better than our regular network," Belinda said.

"That's what I told him," the elder Baxter said.

As the afternoon progressed, both Baxters took turns being the center of conversation—the elder describing the remission of his Alzheimer's, the younger providing details about Brimstone 1 including the upcoming launch window. As the two debated how to announce a specific liftoff time, Elijah and Belinda went to the kitchen to refill the iced tea pitcher and cookie platter.

"What's your major?" Elijah said.

"Peace Studies," Belinda said. "GW has a good program. If you said, 'social justice,' at my old school, it was considered code for 'screaming liberal.'"

"Funny. I always thought Jesus was the original social justice warrior," Elijah said.

Belinda laughed appreciatively. Elijah's phone sounded with a new ringtone he'd uploaded, an instrumental of the Bread song, "Everything I Own." He looked down at his phone.

"Need to take that?" Belinda picked up the tray with tea and treats. "Go on."

Elijah moved to the backyard. The ringtone ended quickly, indicating a text from the contact to whom he'd assigned the old ballad.

JANA: 'Sup?

ELIJAH: At the ranch house, in the backyard. Belinda Moore just flew in. You should come over.

JANA: I'm riding Amyra. Belinda probably wouldn't appreciate it if I trotted up on her horse, even if her father did give me permission.

ELIJAH: Let's get together later.

JANA: Can't. Flight surgeon wants to do one more blood panel. Then I go into medical quarantine for seven days. Standard procedure before liftoff.

ELIJAH: I want to see you.

JANA: Walk past the fire pit.

Elijah went to the far end of the backyard, overlooking the arroyo that had flooded the night of the storm. Jana appeared on the other side. She dismounted and wrapped the reins around the saddle horn. The pair locked eyes across the gulf.

ELIJAH: Hurry back.

JANA: I'll try.

"We interrupt regular programming for a special announcement." Tanya Cummings conducted a live shot from outside the dorms at the space center where astronauts stayed for their pre-liftoff quarantine.

"Brimstone 1 will launch on Palm Sunday, April 13." Baxter was seated inside his dorm, speaking with Tanya via webcam. "We're eager to establish a Christian presence in space, both with the spacecraft itself and deployment of the first cubesats for the Urim communication system."

"When will you return?"

"Good Friday. The orbiter will touch down here at the ranch," Baxter said. A computer animation depicted the landing in a split screen.

Tate yawned dramatically as he and a cluster of Humanist League members watched the broadcast in the main shaft. He already knew Brimstone 1's schedule. Behind him, welding torches glowed, and steel sparked as crews worked on League vehicles.

"How do you like your dorm here at the space center?" Tanya said.

"Very clean and healthy," Baxter said. "And I have a great neighbor."

The window beside the front door next to Baxter's unit went from opaque to clear. Jana waved at the camera from behind the smart glass.

"Commander McAlister, how are you doing in quarantine?" Tanya pivoted toward Jana's unit.

"Doing fine. I appreciate the quiet time to review flight plans and reflect." Jana provided a video feed from her handset. She switched to the rear camera to show the dorm interior, which included a workspace, kitchenette, and digital fitness station. “Baxter is an excellent host. All the comforts of home.”

“Good to hear, commander,” Tanya said. “Let’s go to Church of the Living Waters.” The screen split between Tanya and Pastor Humberto standing in the church sanctuary. “Pastor Humberto Morales, what will be happening at the church during Brimstone 1’s flight?”

“We’re holding prayer vigils twenty-four hours a day from now through touchdown.” The camera panned the vast sanctuary to show prayer groups within the pews and a huge banner over the stage proclaiming “Godspeed, Brimstone 1.” “On launch and landing days, the church campus will be a viewing site with jumbo TVs, worship music, good food, and fellowship. We invite people to celebrate this historic mission.”

“Thank you, Pastor,” Tanya said. “As you can see in the lower part of the screen, Moore Media has started a countdown timer.” The clock graphic activated at T minus 6 days, 15 hours, 33 minutes. “Stay with Moore Media for complete coverage of Brimstone 1, the first Christian rocket.”

Elijah’s class buzzed as the special announcement concluded. Students conversed about going to Church of the Living Water to watch the liftoff. Elijah smiled at their enthusiasm.

“Who’d like to fly on a future Brimstone?” Elijah said. Everyone in the class raised a hand. “Then let’s nail these last equations. The astronaut review board will be impressed.” The class laughed as Elijah turned their attention back to the lesson.

Baxter and Jana held a meeting from their separate dorms. A pane of smart glass in the wall between the rooms activated, with the top portion remaining clear to allow eye contact and other sections acting as monitors. Accessing the Moore archives, they reviewed the longest message of the series, the one received in 1985.

"We estimate The Package was launched in 1979, around the same time this message was sent," Baxter said. "Six years for the radio waves to reach Earth, forty-six years for The Package."

"The Package would have to travel approximately thirteen percent of light speed," Jana said.

"That's right," Baxter said. "After we got the 1985 message, my dad contacted a couple of my grandfather's friends from the Manhattan Project, Luis Alvarez and Richard Feynman. Told them he was producing an outer space movie for the Christian market and needed 'technical assistance.'"

"Quite a brain trust," Jana said.

"They said it would take stupendous energy to reach even a tenth of light speed," Baxter said. "And the payload would have to be incredibly light."

"Rules out a giant spaceship bringing an invasion force,"

"That would've been too *Star Wars*." Baxter smiled. "Dr. Feynman envisioned a micro-ship inside a puff of cosmic dust. He suggested our movie end with it getting sucked into a vacuum cleaner upon reaching Earth."

"How ironic. But those atomic scientists were on the right track. We've seen the photos. The Package seems to have hardly any mass."

"Like I said before, you have to be looking for it."

"The sender asked for secrecy. But you plan to disclose everything."

Baxter restarted the audio file. "I want you, and only you, to receive what I'm sending. I trust you. Let the Spirit guide you, as the Spirit has guided me," the sender said. "Book of John, Chapter 4, Verse 48, 'Then said Jesus unto him, Except ye see signs and wonders, ye will not believe.' No more secrets. Book of Luke, Chapter 12, Verse 2, 'For there is nothing covered, that shall not be revealed; neither hid, that shall not be known.'"

Baxter paused the audio. "Signs and wonders. No more secrets. The sender became an evangelist. We will reveal The Package."

"When?"

"Could be a few days after landing, a few weeks, maybe more. We'll need to secure and study it. We'll need to tell the president."

"In that order?"

Baxter nodded.

At a quarter past midnight, Elijah was at the old desk in his apartment. Conducting his courses was work enough but maintaining the education channel was a huge project as well. As usual, the teaching ministry brought peace and diverted him from looming issues, the largest noted in a special digital folder: The Package.

Both Baxters assumed Elijah knew more about the space object than he did. The elder, convinced that knowledge of the recovery mission had brought Elijah to the ranch, had spoken freely of The Package the night of the storm. Concern that Elijah had learned explicit details drove the younger man to offer him the multi-million-dollar deal. His mutual attraction with Jana, confirmed in the interrogation room kisses, was the intrigue's final dividend.

Elijah's folder for The Package contained only his scant personal notes on the topic. He journaled his latest thoughts. He wasn't going to ask the Baxters or Jana anything more about the mystery. Whatever he knew had been worth twenty-five million dollars, and he didn't want Baxter III to think he'd overpaid. Elijah closed the folder. He would focus on the public-facing Brimstone 1. Any greater revelations would come in their own time with their own lessons.

At half past midnight, Jana lay in bed, legs sore from exertions at the digital fitness station. Like Elijah, she trained her mind on the basics of Brimstone 1, which meant piloting a spaceplane model she'd flown before and retrieving an object from orbit like she did as a young mission specialist in the shuttle's final days. But the object in 2025 was an extraterrestrial creation, not the faulty satellite of 2011. When society learned of The Package, cloistering at Del Redentor would be a blessing. She wasn't the only one who might need sanctuary.

Dawn came on Palm Sunday. Baxter and Jana received a final checkup from the flight surgeon. They moved to the staging room where they donned spacesuits and tested the pressurization and communication ports. Once given the all-clear, the astronauts exited the building.

Moore Media started its live coverage of launch day as Baxter and Jana emerged in the early sunlight. Waving at the cameras, they walked to a waiting convoy of vehicles, taking second-row seats in a Suburban equipped with hoses to pump cool air into the spacesuits. Julius stood beside his Bronco spearheading the convoy. He wore a headset and tactical gear, a Tavor 7 bullpup assault rifle slung over a shoulder. His security squad, similarly equipped, filled three additional vehicles. Once the astronauts were secure, Julius took the wheel and moved out. The procession followed to Rig Alpha.

A security officer drove Elijah to the Church of Living Waters. Protestors lined the frontage road, kept away from the grounds by barricades and sheriff's deputies. The sanctuary was already at capacity with people who had been praying through the night. Food vendors served the throngs gathering on the rolling lawns, terraces, and rocky outlooks. Families spread blankets on the ground, creating a church picnic atmosphere. Portable water tanks on the lawns offered "Brimstone Baptisms." Jumbo TVs throughout the campus showed Moore Media coverage and activities inside the sanctuary.

"Good morning from Church of the Living Waters." Elijah talked into his handset mounted on a selfie stick. "We are waiting for the launch of Brimstone 1. But we have another launch to show you first. Shiloh, one of my students at Jeshimon Academy, has been leading some young rocketeers."

Elijah rotated the camera view, framing Shiloh and a half dozen children standing on a grassy hill. A line of cardboard rockets stood ready, painted with Brimstone insignia, American flags, crosses, and Bible verses.

"We've been learning in kids church how Brimstone 1 works," Shiloh said. "It blasts off using gas made from rocket fuel. We've built rockets that use gas from antacid tablets. And it's time for our blastoff!"

The boys and girls ran to a folding table, grabbing prepared water droppers and antacid tablets. They put the appropriate mix of water and tablets into plastic film canisters taped inside the bottoms of their rockets. They pushed the lids onto the canisters, turned the rocket's nose-up, and set them down carefully. The kids huddled with Shiloh near the "launch site." One by one, the rockets spurted into the air to the cheers of the kids and their families.

"Go Brimstone 1!" Shiloh and the kids yelled in unison.

The convoy stopped at the base of the service tower. A group of technicians ushered Baxter and Jana into the tower elevator, two security members accompanying the astronauts. The assemblage rode to the top. The shiny pillar of Brimstone 1 scrolled past the elevator window, Moore helicopters loitering beyond. The elevator doors opened, and the astronauts and technicians walked across the crew access arm, which resembled an airport jetway. The security members remained on the top level of the service tower, their Tavors in tactical carry position.

The custom-molded chairs in the orbiter rotated forward ninety degrees, allowing Baxter and Jana to assume normal sitting positions while the craft was vertical atop the boosters. Wearing clean-room outfits, technicians connected umbilicals sprouting from the chairs to the spacesuits for pressure and communications.

The president was in the Oval Office. In a few minutes, he would cross Pennsylvania Avenue for services at St. John's. He watched the launch broadcast with his national security adviser.

"Next Brimstone launch, you're getting your surveillance satellite deployed," the president said.

"Sir, the 822nd Base Defense Squadron is currently at Holloman Air Force Base," the national security adviser said. "An advance unit can beef up security at the Moore Ranch. We can easily add more elements for Friday's landing."

"No. We can't be publicly tied to Brimstone 1, much as we want to preserve future launches." The president gestured at the screen. "This is all Baxter's show."

"Brimstone 1, we're at T minus one hour and eighteen minutes." Peter had directed two hours of preflight procedures from mission control. "Booster checks are complete. All systems are nominal. We have a special communication. On your screens now."

A video feed from the sanctuary of Church of the Living Waters appeared on the orbiter control panel. "Hello, Brimstone 1!" Pastor Humberto was in the pulpit. People cheered inside the building and across the grounds. "Our hearts are with you."

"We feel it," Baxter said over his helmet mic. Jana gave the cockpit camera a thumbs up.

"How about some worship music for extra energy," Pastor Humberto said. "This is a new song written especially for the Brimstone 1 mission, 'Heaven's Aflame.'"

The stars of Moore Music took the stage, backed by an eight-piece band, choir, horn section, and strings. 'Heaven's Aflame' was a seven-minute opus with ballad-style verses and rocking choruses. The lyrics combined images of rockets and the Holy Spirit, both propelling God's people with fire. The song ended, and the church crowds erupted in ovation. Baxter and Jana wept. Their chairs rotated upward into launch position.

Elijah moved about the campus, providing livestream commentary, interviewing a former shuttle astronaut who had brought his grandchildren to view the launch. The education channel homepage featured Elijah's livestream, the feed from Moore Media, and an AI-powered media carousel that presented in-depth content on topics discussed in real time.

"T minus thirty-five minutes. Loading propellants," Peter said. Frosty clouds draped Brimstone 1's flank as a super-cooled combination of liquid oxygen and kerosene pumped from the gantry to its tanks.

"T minus fifteen minutes. Go/No go poll," Peter called out the titles of personnel at mission control. One by one, they announced, "Go for launch."

Julius stood in the observation bunker, the closest allowable spot to the rocket. Like Peter's routine at mission control, he quizzed his team leads in a group communication. Ranch gates were secure. Perimeter was quiet. Airspace was clear. Social media and web monitoring detected no overt threats.

"Commander McAlister?" Peter said.

"Go for launch," Jana said.

"T minus two minutes. Propellant load complete," Peter said.

"T minus one minute. Brimstone 1 is in start-up."

"Like the song says, 'Heaven's Aflame.' Light it," Baxter said.

The masses on the church campus went silent, eyes on TV monitors and the hills to the north where Brimstone 1 would rise into view. Shiloh clasped her hands in prayer. She looked away from the hills and saw Elijah standing nearby. He gave her a reassuring smile.

"Ten, nine, eight, seven, six, we have a go for main engine start."

Jana set her body for the coming shock, muscle memory from 300-plus landings on carrier decks and three previous space flights. Baxter held his breath.

"Three, two, one, ignition."

As with the static test, the flame trench filled with exhaust. Building-sized clouds spewed again from the launch pad. This time, the clamps released the fins, and Brimstone 1 lifted off. Cheers ensued from mission control to Church of the Living Waters to watch parties around the world.

The thunder filled the surrounding valley. The old ranch house rattled. This day, Baxter the elder had the foresight to pack his instruments in their cases and remove his mother's china from the breakfront. He stood in the backyard with Belinda and Marta, a protective arm around each. They watched the rocket climb away from the ranch, awestruck.

Brimstone 1 appeared above the hills, a silver needle with a golden thread of exhaust. The church crowd already cheering the televised launch images screamed louder. The roar from more than twenty miles away finally reached them. A sea of cellphones captured Brimstone 1 curving into its downrange arc, an electronic benediction.

"Approaching MAX Q," Peter said.

"Throttling down," Jana said. At T plus one minute, the rocket experienced maximum dynamic pressure, the calculated moment when aerodynamic stresses were greatest. The ship transited the phase smoothly.

"MAX Q complete. All systems nominal," Peter said.

"Throttle up." Jana returned the first stage to full power.

"First stage thrust at 103 percent anticipated level. System updates since static test working better than expected," Peter said.

"You built me a hot rod, Baxter," Jana said. Baxter managed a tight smile as he coped with the g-forces.

At T plus 2:30, downrange over Texas, Brimstone 1 reached MECO, main engine cutoff. A camera inside the fuselage showed the first stage separating from the craft, eliciting more cheers from viewers. Using remaining fuel, the stage descended toward the manufacturer's testing field in South Texas for soft landing and refurbishment. The single booster of stage 2 ignited and continued to lift the orbiter. The ride grew rougher without the dampening mass of the first stage. SECO, second engine cutoff, occurred over the Gulf of Mexico at T plus eight minutes. With the booster's cessation, the g-force effect on Jana and Baxter also ended.

Three minutes after cutoff, the second stage detached from the orbiter. "Second stage separation confirmed," Jana said. The remaining manned component of Brimstone 1 was now 120 miles high, traveling more than 16,000 miles per hour.

"Orbital insertion complete," Peter said. "Congratulations, Brimstone 1."

Shiloh's kids group clustered around Elijah. "Did they make it?" one of the kids asked.

"They made it," Elijah said. The kids jumped up and down.

A plastic model of Noah's ark bobbed at Jana's elbow. She observed an astronaut tradition of placing toys in the cockpit to illustrate microgravity.

"The first ship commissioned in the name of the Lord." Jana nudged the little ark.

"I want to thank the brilliant men and women who made this possible from mission control, ground teams, and our contractor companies. I also want to thank all the people praying for us. We didn't fly up here on rocket power alone!" Baxter turned to Jana. "Let's get to work."

CHAPTER 14

Two-hundred fifty miles above Mauritania, the orbiter's cargo bay opened. A cube the size of a bank vault rested inside, a flexible structure comprising tightly stacked metallic plates, each twelve inches square. Under Jana's control, the robotic arm grabbed a handle protruding from the stacks.

"Cubesat deployment in three, two, one—"

The orbiter's nose pitched down sharply. Cold gas thrusters along the cube's bottom edges activated as the arm lifted. With the three simultaneous actions, Brimstone 1 replicated a medieval catapult, hurling the cube from the hold. The orbiter gently spun end-over-end until Jana stabilized the craft.

The cube began to disassemble, first into a staggered array of stacks, and then into what looked like a cloud of space junk. The cubesats took their final shape, plates separating in twos, electronic guts and housings unfolding between each pair, solar panels extending. In the metamorphosis, the hulking cube became 370 tiny cubes—communication satellites, their ion engines slowly dispersing them like dandelion seeds.

"Therefore, go and make disciples of all nations, baptizing them in the name of the Father and of the Son and of the Holy Spirit," Baxter said.

"Congratulations, Brimstone 1. The first phase of the Urim communications network is underway," Peter said. "T plus twenty-two hours. Let's give you some privacy."

The public broadcast from the orbiter and mission control ended. Instead of going to sleep, Jana and Baxter issued a quick series of commands. A new orbital map appeared on main screens in space and at the ranch. A blue track wrapping Earth represented Brimstone 1. A red track was The Package. Baxter turned up the transceiver locked to the frequency hopping code, and the whoosh of The Package's beacon filled the cabin. The orbiter was giving chase.

"Ten hours, twenty-two minutes to intercept," Jana said.

"Now get some rest," Peter said.

At dusk, a squad of Humanist League members emerged from the main shaft, posing an usually large exposure. Tate directed part of the group to the mine complex's gated entry. A plume of dust rose from the road leading to the complex. Big tires thumped over gravel creating the typical sound of a semi, but the engine note was a less-customary hum.

The bobtail semi stopped inside the gate, futuristic aesthetics rivaling the orbiter's lines. A League member climbed the steps on the driver's side to peer in the cab.

"No driver," said Tate. "I run a lean operation."

The group laughed as Anik directed the autonomous truck from a tablet. The truck backed into a corrugated-metal garage, one of the ramshackle buildings on the site. Inside was a trailer and a hookup to the mine's fuel cells to replenish its batteries.

Tate signaled the second group and motioned toward a nearby pass. A large drone closed at low altitude and landed in an open space near the main shaft entrance. With dimensions comparable to a light sport aircraft, the six-rotor machine was built to haul cargo. League members pulled plastic crates from its belly and ran them into the shaft. The last of the excursion party threw a camo tarp over the drone and connected a line to the fuel cells.

Inside the shaft, League members gathered around Tate and the plastic crates. "Moore and McAlister have their designer spacesuits. I picked out something more fun for our mission," he said.

Members popped the crates to find them stuffed with costumes, masks, and makeup. The garb reflected a half-century of dystopian cinema—*A Clockwork Orange, Mad Max, V for Vendetta, Joker.* People jumped on the flatcar train assembled on the tracks and loaded with armored vehicles.

"We're going cosplay into battle?" a member asked Tate.

"One more way to degrade the enemy," Tate said.

Marissa quietly approached Tate. "I picked the perfect outfit."

"You can model it for me later," Tate whispered.

At two in the morning, Elijah's phone jangled on his nightstand. He read the glowing text:

> **JULIUS**: Mr. Moore requests you at mission control. A car is waiting in the parking lot.

Elijah walked into mission control. Belinda and her grandfather entered from another doorway across the room. Peter and his technicians worked intently in the middle of the night. Julius stood sentinel while security team members guarded the doors. Occupying the main screen, Baxter and Jana tapped commands and monitored readings. On the Earth orbit map, the blue icon for Brimstone 1 was nearly atop the red dot for The Package.

"This better be good," Baxter II said with a wink.

"Two minutes to intercept." Jana made slight adjustments with the orbiter's thrusters.

"Copy, Brimstone 1," Peter said. "Approach on track."

"Some of us know more about The Package than others," Baxter said. "Frankly, we're all ignorant even after eighty years. That's about to change."

"One minute," Jana said.

"You'll have visual soon," Peter said.

Baxter activated cameras and lights at the orbiter's nose. A flicker appeared off starboard, replaced by a streak a few seconds later. The Package's beacon grew louder, a communal heartbeat for the edgy witnesses. The beacon's waveform jagged across screens in the cockpit and mission control.

"Ten seconds," Jana said.

An iridescent ripple interrupted the blackness ahead. Jana inched the orbiter closer, and a bow light pinned The Package. The specter of the lunar images, the voyager of 36 trillion miles was within grasp. Purple pulses etched the matte black surface, a reaction to the orbiter's beam. The luminosity defined a disk forty feet across. The Package nearly disappeared when turned on its serrated edge. Its extreme thinness validated Alvarez and Feynman's low-mass hypothesis. The object began to undulate, conjuring a Spanish Dancer mollusk eluding a threat. Jana blipped the stern thrusters to keep pace.

"Is it alive?" Belinda whispered. Her grandfather shrugged, eyes locked on the main screen.

"Diameter is approximately the length of the orbiter, but it bends." Jana brought the orbiter alongside The Package. Baxter aimed more cameras and turned down the volume on the beacon reception.

"We can fold it into the cargo bay," Baxter said.

"Hopefully, or we'll need a bigger spacecraft." Jana pulled on the haptic glove linked to the claw. "Activating arm."

"Backup controller ready." The robotics technician at mission control showed his gloved hand to the camera.

The arm unfolded from the cargo bay and extended toward The Package. Dual means could capture objects—the mechanical claw for standard grappling as used with the cubesats, and a halo of tethered harpoons for spearing should the claw be unable to gain hold. Jana carefully angled the claw toward the center of The Package.

"It may be easier to gather from the middle than grab by the edge," she said.

Jana advanced the claw in minute increments. She lifted her index finger. In response, one of the claw's grippers raised slightly. Jana moved her finger slowly, and the gripper grazed The Package to test its pliancy. The space object quickly enveloped the end of the robotic arm, the once-flowing shape clumping on the boom. Jana felt the claw shake and contract through feedback to her glove. Her gaze alternated between her hand and the screen.

"Well, if it wants to come home with us that bad," Jana said

"My God, it *is* alive," Belinda said. Her grandfather comforted her with a hug.

"Not necessarily," Elijah said. "Nanofibers can be designed to move like muscle tissue in response to stimulus ... contact, light, temperature."

"Besides, what could live exposed in outer space for almost fifty years?" Baxter II said.

"Something we've never seen. Something Dad's bringing back," Belinda said.

The arm came to a jarring halt after Jana began retraction. She repeated the command to no avail. She tried re-extending without success. Jana shed the haptic glove and issued commands on her touchscreen. The arm remained frozen.

"Mission control, arm is inoperative," Jana said. "Can you override?"

The robotics technician took off his haptic glove and sent commands to the main boom. Peter stood over the technician's shoulder.

"No response," the technician said. The arm remained distended from the cargo bay. The Package was still bundled around the claw, a trailing edge swaying and glowing faintly.

"Requesting EVA," Jana said. Baxter nodded in agreement.

Peter received thumbs up from key technicians. "Commander, you're clear for EVA."

Jana unstrapped from her chair. "I'll try the manual control panel inside the cargo bay."

"And if that doesn't work?" Baxter said.

"I'll inspect the arm for damage," Jana said. "Last resort, I can detach the claw holding The Package and pull it back to the bay."

Jana floated to the rear of the cabin. The bulkhead between the compartment and the cargo bay was a suitport. Two EVA suits were built into the barrier, facing out into the bay. Jana opened a biparting panel, revealing the open backs of the suits. In her "shirt sleeves" uniform, she slid feet first into a suit. The panel closed behind, maintaining cabin integrity. The split backpack united vertically, activating suit power and life support. Jana released the seal that outlined the suit, freeing her from the bulkhead.

Using handholds in the bay walls, Jana moved to the manual control panel at the robotic arm's base. She worked the controls and looked up. The arm stayed rigid, angling out of the cargo bay to where The Package clung to the claw.

"Not responding to manual controls," Jana said. "Heading to claw."

Jana reached for the utility belt built into the hard-shell suit and triggered its thrusters. She paralleled the boom, looking for anomalies to explain the malfunction. She rose to the lip of the cargo bay.

"Don't see any damage." Jana unspooled a tether from the belt and connected one end to a mounted winch, the other end intended for the claw.

Thrusters at dead slow, Jana approached The Package. She had to displace folds to reveal the claw joint for detachment. She gingerly took an edge between her thumb and forefinger.

"It's thinner than Bible paper," Jana said.

"Be careful with it," Baxter said.

"It's stronger than it looks." Jana peeled back a section of The Package to access the claw joint. With her left hand, she turned on a shoulder-mounted light and then felt for a magnetized tool on the utility belt.

Swelling from the other side of the claw, an expanse of The Package arched over Jana like a wave. Viewers gasped as the wave smothered Jana.

"Commander, do you read!" Peter said.

"I'm still here." Jana's breathing was labored.

"Get that arm working!" Baxter said.

Mission control frantically reattempted to activate the robotic arm. The Package tightened around Jana as she maxed thrusters to break free. The claw became visible at the center of the bundle. A coil of The Package yanked her toward the halo of harpoons. Jana crossed her wrists in front of her visor and twisted her body in the opposite direction. A harpoon tip glanced off her forearm. She checked the heads-up display inside her helmet.

"Suit damaged. I'm losing pressure," she said.

Jana jolted and realized the claw was moving. Peter shouted orders at his technicians as the arm jerked toward the cargo bay. The boom abruptly dove, dragging Jana and her shroud across the bay's floor. She cried out as she was pinned, the arm still pushing downward.

Baxter moved to the suitport for emergency EVA. The arm shifted, flinging the claw toward the bulkhead. Jana narrowly avoided being crushed, but the arm tore open the chest of the waiting suit. The impact knocked Baxter from the cabin panel, its vertical sliding doors slamming with a recorded warning of "cabin breach." The suitport seal expanded to fill the wrecked section, per design, but the suit was out of commission. The warning stopped, and Baxter pounded the panel in frustration. He pulled at his IVA suit stowed in the rear of the cabin, the model he and Jana wore at liftoff.

"I can go out the front hatch!" Baxter shouted toward the control panel.

"That suit is not built for leaving the vehicle," Peter said. "You have no thrusters to reach the bay."

Baxter floated back to the control panel, thrashing his arms like a swimmer. Cameras showed the claw wedged in the bay's upper corner, cocooned in The Package. One of Jana's boots jutted from the folds.

Baxter screamed for Jana over the radio link. There was no answer. "Can't we reboot? Kill the power?"

"Circuits are tied to the bay doors. We could cause the whole system to fail. The doors stay open, you'll break up in reentry," Peter said.

Stress built in the arm, and the claw sprang from the bay corner. The boom extended straight up, and The Package remained wrapped around the end with Jana lost within. The arm ignored commands. There was no response from Jana.

Elijah paced as he watched Peter and the technicians huddle at the main workstations. He heard a faint tapping through the babble and occasional shouts. Elijah approached the robotic arm workstation, which was empty as personnel attempted to right the boom through primary orbiter computers. The tap came again.

On the desk, the backup haptic glove jittered, registering feedback from the claw's sensors. The movement stopped and started again, each instance identical in duration and intensity. Elijah's eyes found the pattern as well. One screen showed The Package beacon waveform. Sound muted, the animation represented noise then silence. The glove moved simultaneously with the waveform.

"External interference!" Elijah said. Heads turned as he ran to the main workstations, holding the glove. "The acoustic beacon. The arm is absorbing it. The vibration is making the controller malfunction."

"Sound doesn't propagate through space, teacher," Peter snapped.

"We don't know how The Package works. It could be generating multiple energy types tuned to the frequency," said Elijah. "Send an inverse signal to the controller to cancel the effect."

"That could wipe out all programming," Peter said. "It would take hours to reset."

The arm oscillated, rocking between the cockpit and the tail.

"You're killing Jana!" Elijah said. Baxter II stood beside him.

"Get him out of my control room!" Peter said.

Baxter II prepared a punch for Peter's snarling mouth. Julius waded into the fracas. Audio feedback screeched through the speakers.

"I'm in command!" Baxter boomed over his mic. "Elijah, save her!"

Elijah directed the communications technician to create an inverse signal, the mirror image of the beacon's wave. The digital file was finished in seconds.

"Upload it to the arm controller." Elijah pointed to the digital file icon on a primary screen.

Returning to his station, the robotic arm technician sent the inverse signal. The arm stopped whipping. Elijah held the backup glove by one of its fingers. It no longer moved with the beacon pulse.

"The arm's responding!" the technician said.

The boom collapsed into the bay. The Package slid off the mechanism and hung like a cloud over the orbiter before starting to drift. A fist punched through a gap, then another. Fingers clutched the billows.

"She's still tethered," Elijah said. A camera zoomed in on the line, pulling taut.

Baxter activated the winch and drew The Package into the cargo bay. He closed the overhead doors. The Package went slack, and Jana floated free. She unhooked the tether from her belt and moved to the rear of the cargo bay where Kevlar containers were stored, retrieval vessels for any cubesats experiencing engine failure. With her remaining strength, she began stuffing The Package into one of the containers.

"Let's wrap this up," Jana said hoarsely.

Elijah donned the backup glove to stir the now-docile arm. Extending a gripper on the claw, he prodded The

Package toward Jana. In a few minutes, their combined efforts transformed the sprawling disk into a controlled wad, remarkably compact due to the material's thinness. Jana cinched the Kevlar sac and fastened the bundle to the rear wall. She opened her thrusters to return to the suitport. The spent micro-engines sputtered, and Elijah eased the claw toward her. Jana took hold, and Elijah pivoted the boom toward the crew cabin. Jana backed into the cutout for her suit, the surrounding seal refreshing.

Baxter pulled Jana from the suit and closed the bulkhead. He strapped her into an upright bunk and applied an oxygen mask and vital signs sensors. Jana gulped the air as mission control cheered. Belinda and her grandfather embraced Elijah.

"I knew God sent you to save this ministry!" Baxter II wept.

As they'd practiced, Baxter scanned The Package for microorganisms and radiation. While he and mission control awaited results, the flight surgeon communicated with Jana on a side screen.

"Vitals look pretty good after your wild ride." The flight surgeon reviewed sensor data on a tablet.

"I've had worse," Jana said.

"Rest. That's an order." The flight surgeon moved away from the screen. Elijah approached, tears streaming.

"Remember when I said I didn't need a hero?" Jana cried as well.

"I've had one for a long time." Elijah tapped his heart with two fingers.

"Scan is green!" Baxter announced. "No contamination. No detour to Point Nemo."

Jana tapped her heart to Elijah.

Tate led a sleepy Marissa out of his room at Motel Apocalypse. She still wore the pigtails and extreme makeup of the villainess she'd chosen from the crates. The pair stood in the parking lot, more than an hour before sunrise. Tate pointed at the sky. Amid the ample stars, one point outshone Venus, emerging in the west and speeding toward the opposite horizon.

"That's Brimstone 1?" Marissa said.

Tate nodded. "Make a wish."

CHAPTER 15

The sun climbed over the ranch. Elijah pulled a tripod from his quiver and fastened a small camera. His drones hovered above the mesa, seeking additional angles to capture the orbiter landing. The Bread ballad drifted from his pocket. Upon accepting Jana's video call, an initial screen read, "Urim Network Beta Connection."

"I hope you're not racking up long-distance charges. That's so twentieth century," Elijah said.

"Baxter asked me to test Urim. This is official business." Jana was in the small living area at the rear of the cabin, a privacy screen drawn. Her phone floating at the end of a recharging cable, she donned components of her IVA suit for cabin activity.

"You were right. The shots from here will be unbelievable," Elijah said.

"Touchdown in three hours. The world changes after that," Jana paused. "You may want sanctuary. There's a guest room for you at Del Redentor."

"I have to finish the semester," Elijah said. "Will it be available in June?"

"And then some."

In the cockpit, also clad in an IVA suit, Baxter went through deorbit checklist with mission control. "Reentry program confirmed," he said.

"Ready for aerosurfaces check," Peter said.

Jana took her seat and tested the rudder and elevons for maneuvering in the atmosphere. "Aerosurfaces look good," she said. "Hydraulics nominal."

"Weather window is clear," Peter said. "Minimal cloud cover, winds four knots from the northeast."

"We're coming home," Baxter said.

Elijah chose loitering positions for his drones based on the test video they fed his tablet. His oil exploration system had become a means of enshrining Brimstone 1. A fitting conversion, the secrets of his technology paled against the secrets packed in the spacecraft, and yet they would entwine. Elijah knew he was entangled too, despite the finite terms of his lucrative deal. He re-read the message Baxter had sent him a few hours earlier:

BAXTER: Please think about a permanent position with the Moore organization, and I don't mean teaching at Jeshimon (unless you'd like to keep a hand in it.) You'll always be part of our mission.

Elijah pondered the answered prayer of working for Baxter Moore. Refuge with Jana sounded increasingly desirable. But would there be any escape? They'd be known as the people as who brought The Package to Earth. Another ringtone snapped his brooding.

SHILOH: When will you be at the church?

ELIJAH: Not coming. Working on a special project related to the landing. Have a great time!

Elijah's absence disappointed Shiloh, but there was plenty to do at the Church of the Living Waters's landing celebration. The grounds filled as they had for liftoff. Big screens again blared Moore Media, and a worship team played on an outdoor stage. Shiloh gathered her kids' group, and they watched education channel segments Elijah had prepared for this important day.

"TIG minus two minutes," Peter said.

"Rotating to burn position," Jana said.

Above Norway, Jana swiveled the orbiter 180 degrees so that its tail was facing the direction of travel. Countdown to

TIG, ignition time, continued. Moore Media correspondents explained the procedure in hushed tones during the live feed.

"TIG in five, four, three—" Peter said.

Jana opened the orbiter's main thrusters for deorbit burn. She and Baxter sank into their chairs with the g-force, similar to liftoff. This time, the rockets served as a brake, shedding speed that kept the craft in orbit. The burn lasted three minutes.

"Cutoff in three, two—" Jana shut down the main thrusters.

"Deorbit burn looks good. No need for trim," Peter said.

"Rotating for reentry." Jana turned and tilted the craft's nose, presenting the shielded belly toward the coming heat.

An ambulance raced up the church's main driveway. A preliminary line of sheriff's cruisers blocking the route parted for the vehicle. Wanda and Blue were stationed at a second checkpoint near the grounds. She waved the ambulance to a halt. The driver turned off the sirens as Wanda approached his window.

"911 call. Possible heart attack at the church," the driver said.

"There are three EMT units already on the grounds. One of them would have taken the call," Wanda said. "Please step out, all of you."

The EMTs disembarked as Wanda kept a hand on her sidearm and Blue stood in ready position. Other deputies backed up Wanda, guns drawn. A high-pitched hum split the air, and frantic crosstalk came over law enforcement radios. The autonomous semi-truck from the mine swerved off the frontage road, tanker trailer in tow. State police SUVs assigned to the freeway off-ramp gave chase, but their V-6s strained to match the truck's giant electric engine. The truck barreled through the checkpoint at the base of the driveway, the cruisers still separated for the ambulance's passage. Wanda and the other deputies fired at the cab. The windshield disintegrated, revealing no driver to neutralize.

The truck scattered the officers at the second checkpoint and continued toward the grounds. The intruder left the pavement and plowed across a landscaped rise. People screamed as the truck came over the crest. The cab hit a security fence—stainless-steel cables strung between concrete pylons. The cables sank into the face of the cab as pistons buried beneath the pylons counteracted the truck's momentum. The truck finally stopped, dangling from distended cables. The throngs closest to the intruding vehicle ran.

A metal stalk popped from the cab roof, and several speakers unfolded. "Stay still and quiet or you're all dead!" an ear-splitting voice said. "This tanker is a fuel-air bomb augmented with toxic chemicals. Any attempt to escape, any attempt to disarm will set it off. If the fireball doesn't kill you, the poison gas will."

The crowd keened. Pastor Humberto and his staff urged calm as they moved among the people. Wanda helped the EMTs at the second checkpoint tend injured officers. Determining her fellow deputies were stable, she led Blue up the driveway, her head down. They inched toward the truck.

"We have a list of demands for Baxter Moore," the truck voice said. "Once he lands, he is to proceed here immediately. If he fails to comply, we will set off the bomb."

Jana concentrated on piloting the orbiter over the Kamchatka Peninsula. Red streaks and sparks flickered outside the windshield, normal signs of the atmosphere's friction against the heat tiles. Baxter watched Moore Media's coverage of the truck standoff. Stationed at the ranch runway, Julius occupied a second screen.

"We've shut down the media feeds from the orbiter and the runway," said Julius. "We can talk and move freely. Sheriff's department and state police are at the church," said Julius. He listened to a new development on his headset. "Federal teams en route from Albuquerque and El Paso."

"Send all security to the church," Baxter ordered.

"We can't leave the ranch unprotected," Julius said.

Baxter cursed under his breath. "Bare minimum stays at the ranch. The rest to the church. We won't sit on our hands and hope the government saves our people."

"We can request emergency landing at Spaceport America." Jana referenced the commercial space facility adjacent to White Sands, two hours from the ranch.

"I agree," Julius said. "Keep the orbiter and The Package away from the area. We can stall the attackers. Tell them you'll be there via helicopter."

Baxter shook his head. "When The Package is on Earth, it's at the ranch. Period." He glanced at the Moore Media feed showing social media reaction to the crisis, several of the posts appearing on the sites he'd unwittingly sold to Tate:

> BIG DADDY IN THE SKY, SAVE MEEEEE!
>
> WHY HAVEN'T THEY BLOWN UP THE TRUCK ALREADY? I'M BORED.
>
> MOORE AND MCALISTER AREN'T REALLY LANDING. THEY STAGED THE TRUCK BOMB TO DISTRACT THE WORLD WHILE THEY RELEASE THEIR BIOWEAPON.

Enraged, Baxter split his video call screen and summoned Brad, who was startled by the call from the edge of space.

"Julius, the church, now!" Baxter said. As Julius signed off, he turned his attention to Brad. "Record me and post it everywhere." Brad cued Baxter. "This is Baxter Moore. Brimstone 1 is reentering the atmosphere, and I'll be at Church of the Living Waters very soon. To the terrorists making demands, I'll hear you out. Do not take innocent lives. To the bigger cowards on social media who think this is funny, God help you!"

Tate noted latest developments on his phone as he walked the length of the attack train. "Baxter will go to the church. He's ordered his security there. Do I look surprised?"

"No!" The Humanist League's shout echoed in the shaft. Members crawled over the train in their costumes, checking tie-downs for the armored vehicles and large drones.

Tate's three bodyguards braced themselves near the battering ram on the lead car. Marissa stood on the second car, watching Tate at the end of the train, longing to be beside him. Dutifully taking her assigned place, she hunkered next to a hardened pickup, pistol in hand.

Elijah paced as he watched news on his phone. He felt helpless stuck on the mesa. He saw Baxter's clip and knew the astronauts were aware. A text appeared:

Brad: Are you at the church or the runway?

Elijah: Neither.

Brad: Good.

Shiloh softly led her kids' group in "He's Got the Whole World in His Hands," taking tissues from the outer circle of parents to dry children's tears. The group looked up. A flight of Subaru Bells descended to a Bureau of Land Management landing zone near the church campus. SUVs also filled with security were twenty minutes out, traveling fire roads to the staging area.

Julius jumped from the lead copter and sprinted to the church grounds. "Keep every drone airborne, cover where we're thinnest. Gate and mission control details maintain position. Concentrate everything else on the runway."

With hand signals, Julius directed security members to fan across the grounds. He spotted Wanda and Blue near the landscaped rise where the truck rested. Crouching, he moved quickly to their position.

"Anything new?" Julius said.

"No. The crowd's been incredibly calm," Wanda said.

"I heard lots of praying and singing."

"Do you think the truck has motion detectors?"

"Doubtful. Too easy to set it off. They lose their bargaining chip. Probably using cameras with a human at the detonator button miles away."

"My partner's been calm too." Wanda looked at Blue. "She has the best nose in the Four Corners. If that truck's loaded with explosives and chemicals, she'd react, even from here."

Tate stood on the last flatbed car, his designated command cab. A large plastic skirt spread the width of the car, a seat and control panel at its center. A clear canopy waited to close over the compartment.

"Fuel cells to 110 percent," he ordered.

Anik ran to a relay box beside the tracks. Sparks flew as he turned up the fuel cells deep in the mine. The air buzzed with the current. Anik screamed and flew backward, electrocuted in his final act of obedience. Unfazed by the fatality, Tate took his chair and lowered the canopy.

"Moving out," he said into a headset.

Restrained by powerful brakes, the attack train crawled from the shaft and wound through the switchyard toward the main line.

"Releasing brakes in three, two, one—" Tate said.

The train took the main tracks at terrifying speed. The overloading fuel cells transformed the line into a gigantic rail gun, the magnets on the train's wheel assemblies transferring current from one rail to the other, creating propulsion. League members cried out and toppled. Clinging to a protective plate, Marissa looked back. Tate's car receded in the distance, detached from the train. She reached out, somehow hoping to draw her beloved leader.

Tate calmly worked his control panel. The skirt surrounding his bubble shook and lifted from the stationary flatbed. Rotors bristled on telescoping stalks. Tate's command cab functioned as a cockpit. He hovered over the parked cargo drone that had brought the cosplay elements. His immediate vehicle settled onto the larger machine, latching tight to create an eVTOL, an electric-powered vertical takeoff and landing craft with ten combined rotors. The eVOTL rose above the tops of the steel towers. Tate watched the attack train disappear toward the ranch before he turned south. Soon, he'd be in Mexico where another cell of followers waited.

Julius contacted teams at the ranch. Nothing was seen at the gates, no movement detected along the boundaries.

"Rail spur?" Julius queried.

"Sealed." From the runway, a security officer peered through binoculars at the metal gate closing the spur into the ranch. She glanced at a railroad map on the touchscreen in her Bronco. "No train traffic for twenty miles."

"Send a drone into the canyon," Julius said.

The security officer flew a surveillance drone into the canyon where the main rail line ran. A tiny drone resting on a crag detected the approach and took off. With its cameras pointed downward, the surveillance drone never saw the interceptor diving from above. With the collision, the feed terminated.

"Lost visual from canyon," the security team member said.

"Nothing on the railroad map?" Julius said.

"Nothing."

The surveillance drone had been seconds from spotting the attackers entering the canyon at bullet-train velocity. One League member lost his grip and fell. Others became sick with the violent motions. The gorge amplified the electro-metal shriek, drowning the riders' cries.

"Keep eyes on that barrier." Julius turned to Wanda. "Quiet at the ranch."

Twin thunderclaps sounded. Isolated wails and applause rose from the trapped masses. Those cheering knew the noises were sonic booms from the approaching orbiter, not explosions from the truck.

"We're subsonic, twenty-five miles from the runway," said Jana.

Julius heard the orbiter's audio. "Five minutes out," he relayed to Wanda.

"Meanwhile, law enforcement and security are pinned down here," Wanda said.

Blue was poised for any order, but still uninterested in the truck. Julius and Wanda looked at the dog and then at each other. The pair broke for the truck. Ignoring the agitated radio transmission from her commander, Wanda directed Blue to run ahead and check for explosives. Blue reached the truck and began sniffing. She investigated multiple points along the trailer. Wanda caught up and urged the dog on. The results were consistent: no hits.

Julius struck the side of the tanker with the butt of his Tavor. The metal cylinder resonated, nothing to dampen the strike. He climbed to the cab roof. Parents on the nearby lawn threw their bodies over children. Julius looked down at the kingpin, dislodged and twisted from the truck's collision with the cable barrier. Motioning Wanda and Blue away, he swung his rifle into firing position and sent several rounds into the pin. The tenuous connection snapped, and the trailer rolled sideways and clattered onto a terrace, the sound of a huge, empty tin can.

Julius prepared to send his people back to the helicopters. A text interrupted giving the order:

ELIJAH: Explosion at runway.

CHAPTER 16

Elijah spotted the runway explosion on a drone feed. He looked up to a ball of smoke where a helicopter had been hovering seconds before. He texted Julius. The security officer monitoring the spur gate never saw the large drone that dove straight down on her colleagues. She turned with the flash and felt the heat on her face.

"Chopper five is down!" The security officer gunned her Bronco toward the flaming wreckage. The personnel in the backseat immediately shouldered their rifles, looking for more threats.

A second helicopter took evasive action. The pilot and occupants spotted a weapon targeting them—a latest-generation Kalashnikov drone, bat-winged with a pusher propeller and explosive nose, built for kamikaze attack. The Kalashnikov came head on at 150 knots. The pilot jinked hard left, which put him in the path of another drone obscured by the lead machine. A second explosion, and Moore air presence at the runway was eliminated.

A convoy of Suburbans sped along the runway. The next Kalashnikov skimmed the ground toward the lead vehicle, which swerved. The ones behind did not, and the detonation destroyed two Suburbans. The last vehicle overturned trying to avoid the explosion.

"Are you getting this?" Elijah sent his drone feed to Julius's handset, the only eyes on the runway now with Moore Media coverage shut down and most security units out of action.

"Yes." Julius and the rest of the landing party were airborne again. "All choppers, open side doors, gunner at each. They're using suicide drones. Fire on anything that approaches." The defense was makeshift. The Subaru Bells were not built to be gunships, and security's bullpup rifles were not long-range weapons. Opening fuselages and hugging the ground to mask radar signatures would slow the helicopters' return.

The attack train burst from the canyon and closed on the spur. One Kalashnikov drone remained on a launch catapult, larger than the others with two pusher propellors. League members released the weapon once the train was past the tight canyon walls. The big Kalashnikov sped high over the runway. Its target was downrange.

The orbiter entered the ranch valley, fast and steep. Unpowered in its atmospheric descent, it was committed to the runway.

"Bandit, twelve o'clock, level." Jana picked up the incoming craft.

Tate hadn't completely abandoned his attack force. He remotely piloted the big Kalashnikov from the cockpit of his eVTOL. After putting the suicide drone in a wide turn, he flew alongside the orbiter. This wasn't going to be a quick kill. He wanted to taunt Baxter and Jana before crashing into them.

The battering ram shredded the gate across the spur. At the line's closest approach to the runway, the train jumped the tracks. The grooved steel wheels dug into the ground as the flatbed cars traveled several hundred additional yards. The remaining security vehicles went off-road to meet the enemy. They stopped to form a defensive line, the security officers taking positions behind doors and fenders. The train slewed toward them, gouging dirt and dust into a smokescreen.

Watching the side camera feed, Jana drifted toward the big Kalashnikov. She slid the orbiter's stabilizing fin under the drone's wing. Jana banked sharply, repeating the Spitfire maneuver she'd used against Elijah. The

Kalashnikov tumbled with the contact, the warhead in its nose detonating. Debris pelted the orbiter, but the glide path held.

Tate cursed as the camera view from the big Kalashnikov spiraled before breaking off. "Ground crew, it's up to you."

"Where are you!" Marissa cried as she heard Tate over earphones.

The lead flatbed hit a boulder, ejecting the three bodyguards. The other train cars uncoupled and slid to a halt. Ramps dropped from their sides, and the road vehicles rolled off. The security team opened fire, many rounds ricocheting off armor-plate. The League members returned fire, some shooters hit as they exposed limbs and upper bodies to take aim. The security team thinned the onslaught by a couple of trucks but was soon overwhelmed. The League convoy swarmed past the riddled vehicles, broke through chain link fencing, and rumbled onto the tarmac.

The big Kalashnikov's explosion had knocked out the port camera, but the bow camera still worked. As Jana raised the nose and dropped landing gear, she and Baxter watched the attackers stop their vehicles on the runway at various angles and intervals.

"Can you get us back in the air?" Baxter said.

"Not while we're a glider."

Jana reached for the escape rocket lever in the center of the control panel as the orbiter took fire from the tarmac. She pitched the nose up until the craft was ready to stall, and then pulled the lever. The escape rockets lit as the orbiter stood on its tail over the runway. The blast ignited the League vehicles directly beneath, touching off a chain reaction throughout the others dotting the strip. The orbiter lurched skyward. A few League members ran from the inferno. Two cars at the runway's far end peeled out before the flames reached them.

Elijah watched the assault unfold from his aerie, its distance and complexity dreamlike. He cheered as the orbiter ascended thousands of feet to seeming safety. *They're going to make it. They're going to make it.*

An alert flashed on Jana's touchscreen. The orbiter shook at the apex.

"Escape rockets failing, port side," she said.

Jana coaxed the remaining rockets to overcome the loss of thrust and control. The orbiter dropped. "Losing altitude."

"Can you make it to the emergency pad?" Peter said.

"Negative. I'll have to put her down anywhere."

"We're three minutes out," Julius said. "Choppers 2 and 3 with me to the runway to suppress intruders. Chopper 4 stay aloft. Track the orbiter. Protect astronauts and cargo."

"Orbiter transponder not working," Peter said. "Establish visual contact."

The orbiter gyrated over the ranch, its nose still pointing upward. Elijah anticipated the descent path. As the craft careened toward the mesa, he'd already started sprinting away from the edge. His drones returned to the open quiver on his back.

Run, run. Jana used the stern camera view to steer. The malfunctioning rockets pushed the orbiter toward the rugged hills bordering the ranch, making the mesa her only chance. Jana prayed the flat acreage would provide enough haven for Elijah and the stricken ship.

The orbiter descended at an imperfect angle, landing legs unfolding for its upright landing. The craft nearly smashed into the mesa's rim, scattering a left-behind tripod with its exhaust. Jana wrung one more pulse out of the compromised rockets, straining for altitude to modulate a touchdown. The damaged port units gave an unexpected burst, throwing the orbiter into a high corkscrew.

"No!" Jana called out.

All escape rockets quit, and the orbiter fell onto the mesa, landing legs crumpling with the impact. The craft fell over and skidded to a halt, buckling the fuselage and crushing the cockpit. Elijah emerged from a shallow crevasse. He waded into the smoke and dust. The image belonged in the radio station's pulp sci-fi collection—a spaceship intended to rest neatly on its tailfins instead strewn on an otherworldly plain. The wreck creaked, but the mesa was otherwise silent.

Explosive bolts blew off the orbiter's windshield and the surrounding cowling. Jana became visible, strapped in her chair, covered by a dislodged panel. Her helmet was split, and she was bleeding. Next to her, Baxter's lifeless hand protruded from the cockpit jumble. Elijah ran to free her from the wreckage. She waved him off.

"Cargo bay, back wall." Her voice was fading.

More explosive bolts popped, and the cargo bay doors fell to the ground. Elijah ran to the bay and spotted the Kevlar container holding The Package. He detached the bundle and hurried back to the cockpit. He dropped the container and pulled the panel off Jana. The removal revealed a carbon fiber shard split from the hull, piercing the cockpit. The path went through Jana's thigh, pinioning her to the ship. Gasping, Elijah reached for the projectile.

"Don't. It's keeping me from bleeding out." Jana pointed to the Kevlar container. "The greatest revelation since the resurrection, to use Baxter's words."

A loud hiss escaped the orbiter followed by a noxious odor. Jana closed her eyes with acceptance. "Fuel rupture. Run!"

Ignoring the order, Elijah yanked the restraints on Jana's chair. Mustering a final effort, she tore him away from the straps.

"You're the new prophet." Jana held Elijah's hands. The couple wept.

With a guttural cry, Elijah withdrew from Jana. He stuffed the container into his quiver and ran to the cleft in the rim. The orbiter exploded as Elijah clambered down, the concussion throwing him to the bottom. Metal clanged overhead, and flaming wreckage poured into the cleft. Elijah stumbled from the rocky chute and ran down the trail, the quiver still tight around him.

"Explosion where we saw the orbiter go down," the chopper 4 pilot said.

"Find the survivors," Julius said. Chopper 1 was taking fire from League survivors falling back to the train.

Julius directed his helicopter to the far side of the train. Choppers 2 and 3 dove in to clear the stragglers. Chopper 1 landed, and Julius led its security squad to the broken chain of flatbed cars. The team dispersing, Julius inspected the lead car, still wedged on the boulder that had halted the train. A steel plate from the shattered battering ram fell, ringing loudly. Julius whirled.

The three bodyguards sprang from behind the boulder. Battered from their ejection, guns lost in the churned dirt, they blindsided Julius, making him drop his Tavor. Two of the bodyguards spun him and pinned his arms to the rock while the third collected his assault rifle. He aimed at Julius and pulled the trigger.

"Smart gun. Only works for the owner." Julius smiled while the bodyguard struggled with the locked weapon.

The third bodyguard charged, raising the butt as a bludgeon. Julius stopped him with a front kick and hooked his left leg behind the neck to set a triangle choke. Using his lower body, Julius threw the charger against the bodyguard on his left. That hand now free, he plunged a tiger claw into the face of the last. Julius retrieved his rifle and stepped clear of the unconscious men.

The teams from Choppers 2 and 3 drove League survivors toward the security officers at the train. Some survivors fought to the end, while others surrendered. Julius reboarded Chopper 1 to inspect the runway in a low flight. The smoldering hulks along the strip hurled him back to Iraq, ribbons of desolation as allied airstrikes incinerated enemy ground vehicles along desert roads. Julius spotted someone crawling from wreckage and ordered the chopper down.

Medic kit in hand, Julius ran to the survivor. The victim stopped crawling; the body lay motionless. Julius turned the figure over. Marissa was burned and bleeding.

"We're going to Mexico, right?" Julius looked puzzled as he treated her wounds. "He said most of Moore security had secretly defected and you'd fly us to Mexico after the battle."

"Who said that?"

"Tate. The man I love. The man we serve." Marissa coughed.

"I serve Jesus Christ." Julius's reply was gentle.

Marissa stared at him, shaking her head. The truth swept over her—no defections, no escape plan for anyone except for Tate. Her breaths came rapidly until they stopped. Sirens approached. Two security officers stepped in to perform CPR, allowing Julius to receive the sheriff's department SUVs. Wanda and Blue exited the lead vehicle.

"Crisis teams and the Red Cross on scene to help the crowds," Wanda said. "Feds are diverting to the ranch. They'll be here soon. Governor is mobilizing the National Guard."

Julius nodded. "Chopper 4, report," he said into his mic.

"We're over the mesa. Fire is intense, big blast zone." The pilot brought the chopper closer. "Nothing could've survived."

"Keep looking," Julius said. "They may have gotten out."

The pilot swerved from the smoky column pouring off the mesa. "Toxic plume rising. We have to pull back."

"Gotta keep looking!" Julius ran to Chopper 1. "Take me to the mesa."

"Cap, you heard it's a hazmat scene now," said Chopper 1's pilot. "Nobody's going up there."

Julius shoved the pilot aside, intent on flying the machine himself. Wanda yelled for help. Julius's five best men and women restrained him. Wanda put her face near his, calming, loving.

"You're good," she whispered.

"No!" Julius said. "No weakness!"

"Yes, weakness," said Wanda. "Let the power of Christ rest upon you."

Julius's body finally relaxed. The five security members stepped back. He fell into Wanda's arms.

"Choppers stay grounded. Leave the airspace open." Julius kept hold of Wanda's hand as he slowly left the embrace. "Our ground vehicles are incoming from the church. Place a vehicle with every law enforcement and guard unit. We're guides now. They'll mop up."

By the time Elijah drove from the mesa to the main road leading to the ranch, law enforcement choked the entrance. Osprey tilt-rotors flew in formation, one landing inside the main gate, others heading to the mesa, its summit glowing red. He stopped on the shoulder. There was no way he could pass through the chaos to deliver The Package. A state trooper walked toward Elijah's truck, waving for him to keep driving.

Inside mission control, Julius oversaw Peter and his technicians shutting down programs and equipment. They were implementing Protocol P, a crisis plan to conceal all aspects of the spaceflight dealing with The Package. State and federal agencies were due momentarily.

Peter took Julius aside. "Do you really expect to maintain secrecy if Baxter is no longer here to enforce it?"

"You and your team signed nondisclosures with the Moore Corporations," Julius said. "And corporations do not 'die.' I expect perfect compliance."

Peter wilted in Julius's stare and returned to the mission control workstations. Julius's handheld vibrated with a video call. He slipped into a hallway to answer.

"I have The Package." Elijah was parked on a back road away from the ranch entrance.

"Thank God you made it. The astronauts?" Julius said. Elijah shook his head. "Keep The Package offsite. Too many outsiders to bring it to the ranch."

"What if my friend from the swap meet comes looking for it?"

"Looks like he bugged out to Mexico. I'll try to send some of my team to help you, but we can't afford to draw the slightest attention. Stay clear of everyone in the meantime."

"So I'm on my own?" Elijah said.

"If we want to safeguard and study The Package how the Moores intended," Julius said. "Perhaps we can salvage something from this disaster. I'll be in touch."

As the afternoon wore on, a L-1011 tanker from Spaceport America flew to the ranch, filled with special fire retardant to smother the toxic blaze still burning on the mesa. Passing low and slow, the half-century-old jumbo jet split its belly over the plume. The orange deluge quelled the fire.

Julius cooperated with law enforcement while military personnel and vehicles flooded onto the ranch. He still had one quiet mission to complete—find the mole who betrayed Brimstone 1. One of his officers broke in with a video call.

"Brad Ferris is gone." The security officer was at Brad's office. The door was ajar, his laptop for posting social media updates sitting on the desk along with a half-eaten sandwich.

"You told him you wanted to review updates on the mesa fire for posting?" Julius said.

"Word for word, as you instructed," the security officer said.

"He ran before we could talk to him. We've confirmed our mole." Julius watched surveillance camera footage showing Brad darting from a back door and jumping into his Subaru. Another camera picked him up on ranch dirt roads. Julius sought an additional feed.

"Not seeing a feed from station 12," Julius said.

"Just got word. A National Guard Humvee accidentally struck the installation," the security officer said. "We're blind over there."

"Great," Julius said. "I'll notify the sheriff to pick up Brad. Excuse the cliché, but he won't get far."

Elijah traveled back roads to distance himself from the ranch, trying to avoid authorities. His truck's info system dictated an incoming text:

> **BAXTER II:** Come to my house. We're praying, grieving, worshiping.

Elijah: Who's there?

Baxter II: Belinda and Marta. Some first responders. A bunch of media are staging here.

Elijah: I don't want to see the media right now. They'll recognize me from the education channel.

Baxter II: Understood. Take care.

Baxter II strode to the ranch house porch. He strapped on his cherry-red Strat and spoke into a mic. "We're angry and confused, and the Lord accepts that. Here's a song I recorded about yelling at God, 'Why, Abba, Why?'"

Baxter II started backing tracks on his laptop, replicating the instruments, and backing vocals of the J-Men. He sang and played live with the accompaniment, his voice strong, his guitar fills piercing. News crews viewing the performance reported the side story—Baxter Moore the second, diagnosed with Alzheimer's and out of public view for a decade, was lucid and ministering to a gathering. First responders were rapt, older ones who remembered Baxter II's band weeping. Belinda stood rigid at the edge of the porch, fist pressed against her lips.

Many were singing with the old man by the final chorus. He went into a rubato refrain, just him and his guitar. He strummed a chord and paused. He strummed again and leaned into the mic. His head lowered, and the crowd quieted. Baxter II withdrew his experimental medication from a breast pocket, a million dollars' worth in the bottle.

"Pop, we killed my boy," Baxter II said.

He flung the bottle, pills arcing free into the tall grass. He unhooked one end of his guitar strap. The instrument hit the porch planks with a Hendrix-esque crash of feedback. Marta ushered Baxter II back into the house as he shook his head and sobbed.

CHAPTER 17

Between backroad routes, occasional law enforcement checkpoints, and stops to pray and cry, Elijah's return to Jeshimon Academy took the rest of the afternoon. The campus was dark as attention centered on the ranch and church. He dropped his quiver in a pile of gear he'd collected for a late-semester science fair, a hide-in-plain-sight approach. For now, he was glad to separate from The Package. More separation came in showering away the grime and blood, his and Jana's. More tears came as he braced his palms against the tile. His phone chimed with a video call as he was drying off.

"Can you talk now?" Teri asked.

"Yes, Mom. Like I texted earlier, I'm OK," Elijah said.

"The news just confirmed Baxter Moore and Jana McAlister are gone," Duane said. "We're sorry."

"I had a nightmare last night you were on a mountain of fire," Teri said.

"I told her not to worry. It was just a dream, right?" Duane said.

"And everything happened today, and I thought you were dead too until—" Teri sobbed. Duane put an arm around her waist.

"I have to finish my teaching assignment. Then I'm coming home," Elijah said.

"That's good. Your mother needs you," Duane said. "We need you." The tough man in the wheelchair cried with his wife and son.

Law enforcement and National Guard deployed at the mine site. Bomb-detecting robots rolled into the main shaft. They relayed images of abandoned tools and equipment, the anti-Christian graffiti on the walls. The robots reached the next level, finding the agricultural and living spaces.

"Self-sustaining operation. Obviously well-funded," said the task force lead as he viewed monitors at a tent near the main railway. "They were here a long time."

An alert sounded on the control panel in the tent—methane readings, rising fast. The task force lead ordered a retreat.

Personnel ran from the mine site, many taking cover at armored vehicles beyond the fence. The first explosions were deep and muted, ravaging the lower levels of The Humanist League base. The shaft opening spit rock and flame before collapsing. The spindly steel towers fell in the shockwave.

As the lead sought casualty and damage reports, an officer approached him. "Sheriff's department reporting explosions and fire at an abandoned motel about twenty miles from here."

"We just lost a bunch more evidence," the lead said.

News alerts about the mine and motel explosions appeared on Elijah's tablet. He checked these and other live reports. Christians around the world were holding vigils. Information was coalescing about The Humanist League, its online recruitment and secretive leadership.

Elijah replayed aerial footage of the mine shaft collapse. He thought he heard a different sound mixed with the explosion audio. He muted his tablet. A thump echoed from the gym. Elijah waited, and another came. He shined his Maglite up the narrow stairs leading up to ground level. Concerned about unwanted visitors, he kept gym lights off.

The pile of science gear was strewn. The quiver was gone. Frantic sweeps with the flashlight revealed it several yards from the pile, zipper undone. Elijah shined his light into the opening. His drones were in place but the Kevlar container holding The Package was absent. Another beam sweep found the open container—empty. Elijah heard a swishing in the darkness, then felt rhythmic gusts, like wings displacing the air. Something brushed his face. He cried out and pointed the Maglite upward. A circle of the purple pulses seen in space were inches above his head.

As the rustling crescendoed, Elijah ran for the electric panel and threw on a bank of lights. The Package floated over the basketball court, unfurled, an edge extending over the bleachers. The trembling disk ascended toward the overhead fixtures. Elijah switched off several lights, and The Package settled at a lower elevation.

Elijah's stewardship of The Package could be fleeting if law enforcement or terrorists stormed the gym. He had no idea how or when he could secure transport to the ranch. There was only one thing to do—create an ultimate lesson while the object of study was in hand. He couldn't duplicate the research facilities waiting at the ranch, but that carefully choreographed future for The Package had died with Baxter and Jana.

Elijah retrieved equipment from his apartment. His drones recharged while he organized a workstation at the side of the basketball court. The Package remained aloft in the softly lit gym, occasionally undulating, displaying none of the extreme movements exhibited in space.

Elijah spoke into his phone camera. "I am Elijah Lindstrom, age twenty-six, teacher and engineer. I'm in Todos Santos, New Mexico, on the night of April 18, 2025."

He switched to the outward facing camera to video the disk hanging in midair. "This object was retrieved from outer space by Baxter Moore's spacecraft Brimstone 1. It's codenamed The Package. The Moore family has spent decades and billions of dollars on a secret mission to bring this extraterrestrial artifact to Earth. They did it in the name of Jesus Christ. And in his name, everything I'm saying is true."

Elijah's video was for posterity, not live streaming. He converted his equipment and the science fair gear into a field lab. Elijah made a checklist of Package properties he wanted to investigate:

- Audio signals
- Electric and magnetic fields
- Thermal signatures indicating power source
- Materials composition
- Visual appearance

He programmed two of his drones to fly ultra-slow patterns above and below The Package, videoing every millimeter. Small pulses trailed the drones along the surfaces, a seeming reaction to their presence. He hung a highly sensitive microphone on a boom from the bleachers, tuning out the drones in the connected recording device, much like he canceled vibrations to correct the orbiter's arm.

Elijah adapted his two remaining drones for different types of detection. He swapped the camera on one with an infrared unit to detect thermal waves emanating from The Package, a preliminary step in determining a power source. The drone flew in concert with the first two, their paths calculated to avoid collision. Elijah programmed an electronic camera filter for the fourth drone to visually detect air vibrations, a complement to the mic-seeking audio signals.

A standard radio programmed with the frequency formula picked up The Package's unmistakable beacon, still broadcasting. Elijah set a ring of EMF detectors around The Package to intercept electric or magnetic discharge. Preparing and deploying these devices took hours. He spent more hours adjusting, videoing his immediate observations, and watching readouts on his tablet. At minimum, evaluating the raw data would require months.

Brad sat in Baxter II's cave, where Elijah had sheltered from security. In The Humanist League's hack of the elder

Moore, they'd uncovered a map of the bunker. Brad eyed the Cold War rations stockpile. He was hungry, but not that hungry.

An animal prowled the cave opening, scraping and yelping. Brad brandished his Glock. He could've retreated to the deeper caverns to wait out the intruder. Instead, he ran to the opening, firing before he cleared the tunnel.

Brad's first round hit Blue in the chest. The second hit a sheriff's deputy instinctively peering into the unexpected cavern among the hoodoos. Brad ran for his Subaru parked in an arroyo. Wanda's first round ricocheted off a hoodoo beside him. Her second tore through his leg. Brad took cover behind a stone pillar and returned fire.

"Officers down!" Wanda took position while Brad sent bullets into the blackness.

The shooting stopped and Wanda tended the fallen. Her human colleague had been killed instantly. Blue whimpered, hurt but alive thanks to her ballistic vest. Wanda pulled Blue to cover, and they waited for backup.

Elijah resumed his video journal. "The Package creates an audio signature. It broadcasts radio waves. It moves. It's luminous and reactive. We saw this in space and we're seeing it tonight. It must have a power source and mechanics. I mentioned nanotech to Belinda Moore at mission control. A motive system distributed throughout The Package's structure, microscopic in specific detail ... that's my hypothesis."

One of the drones shot the segment, leaving Elijah's hands free. He pulled down a face shield and climbed the bleachers until he was within arm's length of The Package. "It's time for physical examination and sample collection."

Elijah touched The Package with a gloved hand. "Jana was right. Thinner than Bible paper, measurable in micrometers. I'm feeling a raised pattern on the surface, barely perceptible."

He took off his glove to feel the surface imperfections, then applied a wireless probe to The Package's surface and checked the readings on his DMM app. "No current detected."

Elijah lifted a power tool. "This is a diamond grinder with a dust intake. If The Package isn't harder than the hardest substance we know, I should be able to dislodge shavings. The intake will collect them for further analysis."

He brought the diamond grinder to The Package's edge. "I don't think it's alive. If I'm wrong, I'm sorry. This'll just take a second." He turned on the grinding wheel and applied the lightest possible pressure.

Elijah registered a flash before the gym disappeared. His eyes widened to see Jana's beautiful face. "I'm dead," he said. The Package had hit him with undetected energy when the grinder made contact.

"How can you be the new prophet if you're dead?" Jana gave Elijah a knowing look before moving away.

Elijah pursued her. His feet moved and his chest heaved, but there was no ground to cover and no air to pull into his lungs. He thought he was in space, but the void was white, not black. Only one star was visible, a vast color spectrum pouring from a single point of light.

"You can't come with me," Jana said.

"I love you," Elijah said.

"I love you, even more than when I last saw you," Jana said. "But you belong in the world, or I should say worlds." She turned again to leave.

"What's going to happen?"

"What you make happen as part of God's plan."

A man's hands came from behind Elijah to clasp his shoulders. He knew who had approached him. Elijah turned to face his Lord and Savior. The clasp tightened with a jolt.

Elijah was at the bottom of the bleachers. The wheel of the diamond grinder was shattered. A strange mark filled his palm resembling a starburst. Elijah touched the mark with his opposite hand—perhaps an electrical burn, but there was no pain. He rolled to his side, trying to clear his head and stand. He came to his feet quickly when he saw Brad limping toward him, a bandana tied around his wounded leg. Brad focused on the disk floating in the gym, flickering purple in the early sun coming through the clerestory windows.

"The Package. So it is real," Brad said. "And it survived, even after so many people died on your side and mine."

"You said it was good I wasn't at the runway. Now I know why." Elijah indicated The Package with a sweeping gesture. "You want to tell that maniac at The Humanist League about this?"

"Just before I shoot him. He saved his own butt while he sent everyone else to die and left me to rot," Brad said. "Did some heavy off-roading getting off the ranch and broke an axle. I need your truck."

Elijah replied profanely. Brad pulled the Glock.

"Tonight, I graduated from a craven spy to stone-cold killer," Brad said. "Keys, bro."

Tires screeched outside the gym building. "Brad Ferris, this is the FBI," a voice said through a bullhorn. "You're surrounded. You and anyone else in there, come out with your hands up."

Brad looked past The Package to a roof hatch in the corner of the gym. He struggled up the bleachers to the ladder leading to the opening. He threw open the hatch and climbed on the roof. Elijah raised his hands and pushed open a door. Outside, agents ordered Elijah to walk backward toward them and lie face down. Brad ran down the gym's arched roof, shooting. He cried in pain as he jumped to a supply building. An M4 round caught him mid-leap.

As agents hurried to where Brad fell, Elijah turned his wrist slightly to look at the drone feed on his watch. The Package undulated and rose, turning translucent in shafts of sunlight, curling into a tube, and floating out the open hatch, the drone giving chase. Once in the open air, The Package resumed its disk shape and spun like helicopter blades, nearly invisible and unnoticed by the federal SWAT team. The Package pulled away from the drone in a vertical trajectory, the silent coda to Brimstone 1's fiery rise and fall. Agents hustled Elijah to a government SUV. He craned his neck to see Brad's body in a pool of blood. Elijah wept for all the losses of the past twenty-four hours.

The President of the United States watched developments from New Mexico in the Oval Office. The national security adviser and White House chief of staff watched his anger.

"I told Baxter he needed better security," the president said. "Any more on this Humanist League?"

"They had a mole in the Moore organization, just killed in a shootout with FBI SWAT." The national security adviser put a folder on the president's desk. "We're building a profile on the leader. Tate Burrell, thirty-three, led a failed start-up in Silicon Valley about ten years ago. World-class expert in AI and digital psychology. Presumed in Mexico now."

"Chase him to the gates of hell," the president said. "Anything else?"

"We're getting scraps of intel that Baxter Moore had another purpose for Brimstone 1," the national security adviser said.

"Beyond our special payloads?" the president said.

"He was recovering something in space. Something alien."

"Sounds like one of those conspiracy theories Sen. Fairchild was screaming about," the chief of staff said.

"It's more credible than that, but still unsubstantiated," the national security adviser said.

"And it will stay that way," the president said. "The more people dig into Brimstone 1, the more we risk exposing our lift program. We know our prime suspect. He has an anti-Christian agenda. His insider accomplice is dead. Most of his close followers are too. That's enough for me. That's enough for our evangelical voters." The president turned to his chief of staff. "Get me the AG, Secretaries of Defense and Homeland Security. I want investigations tightened up. No going down rabbit holes. If anyone sends me a UFO report, they'd better attach a resignation letter!"

"So you were working all night on a science fair?" the FBI agent said. "Isn't that unusual given recent events ... one of the biggest terrorist attacks ever on American soil, a multibillion-dollar spacecraft destroyed, dozens dead?"

Elijah sat before the agent in a trailer on ranch grounds, a mobile office for federal law enforcement. "That's exactly why I was working, to take my mind off it."

"And Brad Ferris just shows up," the FBI agent said. "You weren't talking to him earlier? Maybe helping him out? That's what friends do, right?"

"A real friend doesn't pull a gun on you. He was stealing my truck."

"How about during the day?" the agent continued. "Did you and Mr. Ferris have contact? Where were you during the attack?"

Elijah had no cover story for his whereabouts when Brimstone 1 crashed. He either had to tell the truth, lie, or demand a lawyer. Another agent entered the mobile office and pulled the interrogator outside. Alone, Elijah prayed in the quiet.

The second agent reentered. "Mr. Lindstrom, that's all the questions we have. Thank you for your cooperation. We know this has been traumatic."

A federal vehicle dropped Elijah at the campus. He received permission to enter the gym as the crime scene was outside. The drones had returned to the quiver, triggered by Elijah's sudden movements when the FBI took him away. His tablet showed all files had automatically closed and been concealed, no compromises of the device or contents detected.

Julius arrived with three security officers. “Broke free as soon as I could. Heard you had a chat with the feds.”

Elijah reached into the gear pile. He held open the Kevlar container, its emptiness speaking loudly.

“Do they have The Package?” Julius said.

“Nobody has it now,” Elijah said.

The container slipped from his fingers. Julius caught Elijah as he collapsed.

CHAPTER 18

"How is he?" Elijah said.

"Good days and bad." Marta closed the ranch house door behind Elijah. "He'll be glad to see you."

Elijah set down his gear bag as Marta offered iced tea and cookies, reminiscent of the happier gathering before the launch. Elijah sipped as Belinda entered the room.

"Nice speech you gave today at the academy commencement," Belinda said.

"It's been rough on the students," Elijah said. "Everyone was given the option of accelerated online courses after what's happened. They also voted to have an online graduation ceremony."

"It's been rough on everyone." Belinda poured herself some tea.

"Are you going back to DC to finish your bachelor's?" Elijah said.

"No need. GW provided an online option too. I'll have my program wrapped up in a few weeks. No big graduation gala for me either."

"What's next?" Elijah said.

"I'm America's newest billionaire. I don't get control of the Moore enterprises, but I do get enough money to keep me happy and quiet. I hear you got a sweet deal also. My father was always generous in his special way. Now that you're happy and quiet too, how will you realize your potential?"

"I have some plans."

"That sounded drab. But this isn't a time for celebrating. We've all lost people we love. The tall blonde riding my horse that day. I figured out she was Jana the astronaut."

Elijah shot Belinda a look.

"I'm sorry," she said.

"Likewise." Elijah set down his tea, grabbed his gear bag, and headed upstairs.

The man under the sheets in Baxter II's room looked much more like the Alzheimer's patient he'd been in previous years. Elijah sat bedside and took his hand.

"I'm going to be out of range. You should have this back," Elijah placed the walkie-talkie from his gear bag on the nightstand. "Thank you for making me part of your ministry."

A tear rolled sideways down the old man's face.

Elijah loaded the last of his belongings into his truck. He'd been the only regular presence on campus for weeks, and that was ending. A devotion appeared in his email feed, 1 Corinthians 3:10–15:

Because of God's grace to me, I have laid the foundation like an expert builder. Now others are building on it. But whoever is building on this foundation must be very careful. For no one can lay any foundation other than the one we already have-Jesus Christ. Anyone who builds on that foundation may use a variety of materials—gold, silver, jewels, wood, hay, or straw. But on the judgment day, fire will reveal what kind of work each builder has done. The fire will show if a person's work has any value. If the work survives, that builder will receive a reward. But if the work is burned up, the builder will suffer great loss. The builder will be saved, but like someone barely escaping through a wall of flames.

The flames had come, and Elijah had escaped. He wondered if he'd built anything lasting. He wondered if he could rebuild a mission and a life. As he drove through the school security gate, a throng of students led by Carla waved from the side of the road. They unfurled a banner with the headline, Thank You, Mr. Lindstrom, encircled with personal written messages. Elijah pulled over and exchanged emotional hugs with his headmaster and students.

"Don't know what I'll do without the robot overlord," said Shiloh.

"I'm looking at the real robot overlord at Jeshimon," said Elijah. "Maybe I'll report to you some day."

Later that week, an audience sat inside the completed indoor arena at Del Redentor surrounded by photos of Jana on easels. Construction was active across the ranch, with the other buildings transforming into Jana's VR rendition.

"We appreciate everyone who believed in our daughter and her dream," said Mrs. McAlister into a microphone. Her husband, Dr. McAlister, stood beside her, holding her hand. "Del Redentor is coming to life as you see. Thank you for your generous gifts and support. Special thanks to the Baxter and Marjorie Moore Foundation for grants to complete construction and start the endowment that will keep this place of healing open for decades to come."

After the speech, people waited to give best wishes to Dr. and Mrs. McAlister. During Elijah's turn, Mrs. McAlister took his face in her hands and kissed him tenderly.

"Dear Elijah," Mrs. McAlister said. "Jana spoke of you often."

Elijah walked a trail leading away from Del Redentor's main complex. He was alone until Julius stepped from behind an oak.

"Nicely done with the grants," Elijah said.

"As the new executive director of the Moore Foundation, I'll make sure we give as Mr. Moore intended," Julius said. "The foundation has also received majority control over Moore interests. I'm stewarding his vision there too."

"Sounds like you'll be busy."

"I'm giving myself a proper holiday first. Blue's recovered, and Wanda needs a break too. I'm taking her home to England. I've picked out a perfect spot in the country to propose."

"May not be anyone's idea of a wedding present," Elijah pulled an external hard drive from his gear bag. "Every file I made on The Package that night."

"We'll get to work on this," Julius said. "Quietly. Slowly. We've avoided deep government scrutiny so far, but there will be future administrations, lingering questions."

"We have our own questions to answer. I just enhanced this video." Elijah showed Julius his tablet screen. "I felt tiny irregularities on The Package's surface. I worked with the video sharpening."

Elijah manipulated the image. The closeup of The Package's surface showed a dense array of symbols in sudden relief.

"Looks like writing," Julius said.

"I thought it was lines of code at first. Then I found this." Elijah called up a closeup of another section and adjusted the image. There were more tiny raised markings, a more familiar configuration:

Ye are the light of the world. A city that is set on a hill cannot be hid. Neither do men light a candle, and put it under a bushel, but on a candlestick; and it giveth light unto all that are in the house.

"Matthew 5, 14 and 15," Elijah said. "The entire King James Version is etched in the surface of The Package. My preliminary analysis says the other group of symbols is a part of a translation."

"An alien version of the Bible?" Julius said.

"Put a digital linguist on this. Among its many secrets, The Package is the equivalent of the Dead Sea Scrolls and the Rosetta Stone." Elijah wept. "I'm sorry I lost it for you."

Julius held up his mobile device. The beacon whooshed over the speaker. "Live transmission, relayed from the ranch. The Package returned to Earth orbit and has stayed there. It's not lost." He put a powerful, reassuring hand on Elijah's shoulder.

"Mr. Moore asked you about joining the organization permanently," Julius said. "The offer stands."

"Will there be a Brimstone 2?" Elijah said.

"Eventually."

"You'll need a pilot."

Teri stood outside her garage in Williston, covering her eyes to receive a surprise. The door rolled up. Elijah walked onto the driveway, followed by his father. Duane's wheelchair was set aside. He walked as well, legs clad in an exosuit resembling lightweight braces, a cap sending brain impulses to the electric motors. Teri screamed with delight as Duane made his way into the sunlight.

"Hold still, cutie. I can't handle a moving target yet." Duane walked to his wife and kissed her soundly. "Hope you don't mind if me and the boy run off for the day, and I do mean run." Teri smiled and nodded, and Duane kissed her again.

On the last day of paddlefish season, Elijah and Duane stood on the bank of the Missouri River, their favorite spot when Elijah was a boy. Duane maintained his balance as he cast a ten-ounce hook into the cloudy flow. He and Elijah kept casting and drawing back the hooks, trying to snag one of the unusual-looking fish returning to spawning grounds.

Duane patted his exosuit. "Insurance doesn't cover a gadget like this."

"No worries." Elijah flung his hook again.

"Probably comes with a bigger mortgage than our house," Duane said.

"You don't have a mortgage on your house," Elijah said. "I stopped by the credit union this morning and paid it off."

Duane let his line slacken. "What were you really doing in New Mexico?"

Elijah looked at him but didn't answer. The secrets and subsequent spending chilled Duane. He knew Teri's nightmare about his son being on the mountain of fire was close to reality. Duane's line jerked, and he reeled in his catch. A paddlefish lifted from the water, looking like a prehistoric creature with its long, flat snout. Elijah helped Duane cradle the sixty-pound catch, the Lindstrom men whooping.

A week later, Elijah packed his truck. Teri and Duane looked on from the porch, holding each other, tears flowing. The front of Duane's sensor cap sported a University of North Dakota patch.

"Two video sessions a week with the bio-mechanical therapist." Elijah said. "Mom, don't let him be ornery."

"When will we see you again?" Duane said.

"Not for a while," Elijah said.

Teri smothered her son in a hug. Elijah looked Duane in the eye as he stood an equal six-three again. Father and son hugged for the first time in years.

Elijah headed east on North Dakota Highway 1804 toward US 52—destination Fargo. With hours to go, he opened the podcast app on his truck's info system. Atop his suggestions queue was an episode about using nanorobots in oil exploration. He'd never heard of the podcaster, "Deep in the Borehole." Elijah selected the offering. After a few seconds of silence, an electric guitar blasted the speakers. Elijah jumped.

"That was audio of the Stratocaster drop during the ranch house jam. Wish I had a recording of the orbiter explosion," Tate said over the speakers.

Elijah's mind raced. He'd covered his tracks over the past weeks, altering mobile device records to obscure his presence at the mesa, encrypting messages and calls, setting up an LLC to receive payment from Baxter's estate.

"I assume this is a live stream," Elijah said.

"Of course, and you're on the air with me," Tate said. "Analyzed every possible keyword to make my production irresistible to your algorithms."

"Impressive how the world's most-wanted man gives me so much attention."

"I still want you on the winning team. I know you're leaving Williston. The file has a geotracking feature. Make a left turn for Canada. You can be in Vancouver tomorrow. I have people there. They'll send you to me."

"Brad was coming for you. I can pick up where he left off."

"That doesn't sound very Christlike. You're obligated to forgive me. Those are your rules."

"It'll be easier when I'm standing on your grave."

"Wow! I turned you into a crusader, a bloodthirsty Christian."

"I'll beat my sword into a plowshare when this is over."

"And when will that be?" Tate said. "The crusades lasted a long time. Keep looking over your real and virtual shoulders. Next week ... twenty years from now ... I'll be there." Transmission ended with static.

That afternoon, Elijah arrived at the Armed Forces Recruiting Center in Fargo. Chief Petty Officer Lopez, the recruiter, ushered him into his office.

"Mr. Lindstrom, good to see you," said CPO Lopez. "I passed on the information you sent me. Not to get too far ahead of ourselves, but people in Pensacola are eager to meet you. All fans of your education channel and the work you did with the late commander. She'll always be a great hero to us."

"Me too. It will be an honor to follow her path," said Elijah.

"The path begins at Officer Candidate School and then goes to flight training. The rest is up to you, including application to the astronaut program once you prove yourself with jets," said CPO Lopez. "You plan to fly as high as Jana McAlister did?"

Elijah nodded. "And touch the face of God."

###

ABOUT THE AUTHOR

Jason William Karpf grew up with storytelling. The son of a screenwriter, he was a child actor in the early 1970s, appearing on classic TV shows *The Bold Ones*, *The Courtship of Eddie's Father*, and *Bonanza*. Screenwriting became his calling from his teens to early thirties. In 1994, he wrote the book *Anatomy of a Massacre*, the true story of the era's worst mass shooting.

Today, Jason is an author, speaker, college instructor, and marketing/fundraising professional. His blogging and nonfiction writing brings a Christian perspective to marketing and communication. His science-fiction and thriller novels put Jesus first.

Jason and Ann, his wife, live in Minnesota and have three grown children. When he is not writing, speaking, or teaching, he is making music, playing in the worship team of his church. A history and trivia aficionado, Jason was a four-time champion on the TV game show *Jeopardy*.

Made in the USA
Monee, IL
29 November 2021

82917911R00129